Bob Moats

I0567275

Fatal Abductions

By Bob Moats

Rev. 0719141153a

1

Fatal Abductions

This is a work of pure fiction. Names, characters, places, and incidents either are the product of the author's imagination or are used fictitiously, and any resemblance to actual persons, living or dead, business establishments, events, or locales is entirely coincidental.

For information and address:
Magic 1 Productions
P.O. Box 524, Fraser MI 48026-0524
Website: http://murdernovels.com
Cover by Bob Moats

Bob Moats

Extra special thanks to:

Special thanks to Val Brooks who edited this book
and for her great suggestions.

Thanks to the beta readers Cindy Gross Valstad,
Susan Houghton and Al Norris.

Thank you to all the people who purchased this book.
I hope you enjoy it as much as I enjoyed writing it for
my faithful readers.

The Jim Richards Family of Readers is listed in the
back of the book.

Fatal Abductions by Bob Moats

Chapter 1

Alex ran through the woods, hiding from his brother.

Jeffrey called out to his older brother, "Come on, Alex, don't do this. Mom will be mad at you for leaving me alone out here. Come on, Alex, come back. I'm scared."

Alex laughed to himself so he wouldn't give his position away. He quietly came up right behind his little brother, hiding behind a tree. He watched the eight year old standing in the dim light of the moon and start to cry. Alex had a history of getting in trouble and for a sixteen year old, he had seen his share of doing things the way he wanted.

Alex and Jeffrey lived with their mother, since their father was in prison for murder. Alex was a lot like his father, short of murder. Jeffrey was more like his mother.

Jeffrey yelled again, "I'm telling Mom on you! Come back here and take me home! Now!" He stamped his foot and broke a couple twigs. The snapping was loud and scared the young boy.

Alex was just about ready to step out from behind the tree to scare the bejeezus out of Jeffrey when a very bright blue beam of light shone down from above on the young boy. Jeffrey looked up but had to shade his eyes to see.

Alex snapped his head up to see where the light came from. He looked into the light and it nearly blinded him. He had to avert his eyes to see. When he could look out again, Jeffrey wasn't standing where he was a few seconds ago. He was gone and so was the light.

~~*~~

Sarah rolled over and nearly pushed Van Gogh off the bed. The dog rolled away and jumped off the bed. He sat up on the floor at the edge of the bed giving Sarah a stare that told her she wasn't loved right now. Sarah giggled at the dog and swung her legs over the edge to get up. Her husband, Sheriff Dave Chandler, had already left the house to go to fight crime in the small town of Brinnon, Washington.

Sarah went into the bathroom and did her morning routine. Van Gogh yawned and watched her from the door. She came out, went to the kitchen and got a bowl of food for the dog. Van Gogh wolfed down the chunks of food as Sarah made breakfast for herself.

On the kitchen counter she saw the note. She picked it up, read it and smiled. Dave liked to leave little love notes for her and this one was especially nice. She folded the note and slid it into her jeans. She'd pull it out later that night to remind her husband what he said.

Fatal Abductions

She went to the desk Dave had set up for her in the living room where she could look out the floor to ceiling windows at the waters of Hood Canal. She sat and placed her glass of juice on the desk then started up her computer. She had finished writing her last book about the terrorist who tried to spread a virus that turned people into...well, she didn't want to bring up the zombie thing again. Dave was trying to get over tourists wanting to see zombies around the area. He tried to downplay the fact that good citizens had died because of the virus and it didn't turn them into the walking dead.

She was now starting to write about her last adventure with her new friends, Penny Wickens and Jim Richards. The couple came up from Las Vegas on vacation and they ended up stopping a threat of a new drug that would kill a lot of people. After saving the world, Jim and Penny visited with Dave and Sarah for another few days and then went back to Vegas.

Sarah sat staring at the screen of her computer and wondered what exciting new adventures she and Dave would have. It seemed that since she moved from New York to Brinnon, her life was filled with serial killers and terrorists. She hoped nothing would disturb her now quiet existence.

Her phone rang and she jumped. She picked up the phone and said, "Hello?"

"Hey, honey, are you finally out of bed?" her husband asked.

"Yes, I am. I'm at my desk and working. Or trying to. Anything dangerous going on in town?"

"Just speeders and complaints about noise. Seems a few young people in the new apartments up at the north end are having an early morning party. I sent Virgil to take care of it, but I'm afraid he may end up joining the party. If he doesn't come back in an hour, I'm sending Mike."

"If that's the worst you can come up with, I guess the town is safe. I got your note," she said, smiling.

"Did you get the meaning of the message?" he asked.

"I'm sure I did, you naughty boy. You'll regret that suggestion."

"Fine with me. Now I have to go, Mike just came in and I have to get to work. Talk later," he said and hung up.

Sarah hung up and sat back. She looked at Van Gogh and said, "Want to go out back and chase a few squirrels?"

Van Gogh seemed to understand and was bouncing. Sarah got up and went to the door to the back to let the dog out. She followed him and went to the breakwater of the canal at the edge of the backyard. She loved to look out at the water and remember the busy, dirty streets of New York where she grew up. She liked here better.

~~*~~

Fatal Abductions

Dave stood as Mike, his deputy, came up to the counter. "Mike, can you watch the office for a few minutes while I go get some snacks and coffee?"

"Sure, Chief. Where's Virgil?" Mike asked.

"He's breaking up a wild party. If we don't see him in an hour, you'll have to go arrest him and the rest of the partiers."

"My pleasure," Mike said with a smile.

Dave came around the counter to go out, but the front door opened and in came Mrs. Halpern and her son Alex. Dave stopped to see what trouble Alex got into this time.

"Dave, you have to help. Jeffrey is missing," she said excitedly, coming up to the sheriff.

"Calm down, Agnes. What happened?"

"Alex and Jeffrey were out playing in the woods behind our house and Jeffrey got lost in the woods. Can you start a search?"

"Okay. First let me talk to Alex to see what happened. Alex, come around here and sit at my desk."

The boy reluctantly went through the swinging half door to the chair next to Dave's desk. Dave told him to sit.

"Now, Alex, what happened?" Dave asked the boy.

Alex was quiet for far too long. "Alex, if you know what happened to Jeffrey, you need to tell me," Dave said.

Alex said quietly, "I don't know."

"Were you with Jeffrey when he disappeared?" Dave asked.

Alex sat without saying anything again.

"Alex, you have to talk if we want to find your brother."

"He's gone," Alex finally said.

"Gone? Gone where?"

"He disappeared in the light."

"What light, Alex?" Dave asked.

"The light from the sky. It came down and took Jeffrey."

"Are you saying some light grabbed your brother and took him?"

"That's what I said!" yelled Alex. "Didn't you hear me the first time?"

"Okay, Alex, calm down. I just need to know, what kind of light was it?"

"A bright blue light. It got on him and he was gone. I didn't see where he was taken. The light was too bright for me to see. It had to be aliens! They got Jeffrey!" He was getting hysterical.

Fatal Abductions

His mother was standing behind him and hit him on the back of the head.

"Don't lie to the sheriff! What happened to your brother?" she screamed.

Dave looked at her and said, "Agnes, calm down. Let me take care of this."

The woman backed away from her son and the sheriff and stood by the counter. "Make him tell the truth. He probably did something to Jeffrey that made him run away. Jeffrey was a good boy, not like this disgrace of a son."

"I'm telling the truth!" Alex yelled. "It was a light that took him. It had to be aliens. I saw the light and he was gone. I may be bad, but I wouldn't do anything to hurt Jeffrey. So stop saying that, you old witch! You never liked me anyways." The boy started to cry.

Dave stood and went to the woman. "I think you should go out to the lobby and sit while I talk to the boy."

"You gonna listen to his lies? He probably hurt Jeffrey and the poor child is lying hurt in the woods. You need to start a search," she wailed.

"I intend to, Mrs. Halpern. You just need to sit and relax while I find out what happened. Now go sit out in the lobby." Dave looked at Mike and motioned him to take the woman out. Mike came to her and gently guided her away from the counter.

Dave went back to sit by Alex. "Okay, start at the beginning. Why were you two in the woods?"

"We were playing. I hid from my brother but I was watching him. I didn't want anything to happen to him. But then this light came down from the sky and he disappeared. It had to be aliens."

*

Chapter 2

Dave turned to Mike standing at the counter looking skeptical. "Mike, call all the volunteer search people and go organize the hunt behind Agnes' home. I'll bring Alex with me to get us on the right track."

"Okay, what about Virgil?" Mike asked.

"Give him a call and see where he is. Tell him to scare the crap out of the party goers and join you in the search."

"I'm on it," Mike said and went to his desk to call the people who had volunteered to help in searching for persons who got lost in the forests around the town. He called Virgil first and explained the situation.

Fatal Abductions

"Okay, Alex, I want you to show me where you last saw your brother. Can you do that?"

"I think I can. Do I have to go with my mother?" he asked.

"No, you'll go with me. I'll send your mother home in case your brother makes it back to the house by himself." Dave stood and went out to the lobby. "Agnes, I need you to go home to wait and see if Jeff goes back home on his own. Do that for me, please."

The woman stood. "What about Alex?"

"I'll take care of him and have him walk me through what happened in the woods. Just go home and wait. I'll call if we find anything."

"Thank you," she said and went out the door.

Dave went back to Alex and said, "Now can you remember where you were when you saw this light?"

"I'm pretty sure I can find it again. It wasn't too far from the house. I'd never take Jeff into the deep woods," he said.

"Okay, let's go," Dave said to Alex, then turned to Mike. "I'll be out in the woods. Have everyone meet us there. Call my cell when you get there."

Dave took Alex to his Bronco and they drove out to where the boy lived.

"There's a Forestry service road just before my house. Turn there," Alex said.

"I know the road. It used to be used by couples to go and…well, they'd park out there," Dave said with a grin.

"They still do. I used to creep up on them and scare the hell out of them. I almost got shot one time by some guy in a pickup with a shotgun." Alex laughed.

"Do you know who that was?"

"Nope, never saw him before or after. He was with another man, though, so I don't think he was parking."

Dave said under his breath, "Never can tell."

They arrived at the service road and Dave drove down until Alex told him to stop. They got out of the car and Alex led Dave into the woods not far from the road.

"My house is just over there," he said, pointing. "About 500 yards. I used to come out here to watch the stars. There's a clearing ahead where you can see them real good. We were just next to the clearing when Jeffrey was hit by the light."

"Have you ever seen lights out here before?" Dave asked.

"Just from hunters. But they are low to the ground. This light last night was straight up." Alex stopped and looked around. "It was about here that it happened. After Jeffrey disappeared, I hunted for him. Then I got scared and ran back to the house. Mom wasn't home. She has a boyfriend that she spends a lot of time with. She didn't come back until this morning."

"Why didn't you call her last night? After Jeff disappeared," Dave asked.

"She wouldn't give me the number. She didn't want me to bother her while she was with her boyfriend."

Dave thought about questioning Agnes about this. Maybe have the county children's protective service look into it.

Alex stopped again and looked around. "It was here. I hid behind that tree there when the light came on."

Dave walked around the area looking at the ground. He saw a number of shoe prints in the dirt, some small, some big. He'd need a forensic team to cast the prints, but the nearest was the state police post. He didn't want to get them involved if this was just a case of a frightened child who ran off.

Dave's cell phone rang and he answered after looking at the caller ID. "Mike, I'm just off the Forestry road. You'll see my car. Yell when you get here." He hung up.

"Alex, what kind of light was it?"

"Really bright. Like one of those spotlights that they use to promote some event. It was narrower than one of those big lights, smaller."

"Think back, did you hear any noise from up above? Where the light came from?"

Alex tried to think about what he had heard. "Yeah, it was a light whooshing sound, like a fan on low."

"Propeller sounds like from a helicopter?" Dave asked, looking up at the tree tops.

"No, I've heard helicopters before at the state fair, and they're much louder. This was a lot quieter."

Dave could hear Mike yelling in the distance and yelled back to follow his voice. He kept yelling and finally Mike came into the area with Virgil and five other men.

"Thanks for coming, guys. We have a young boy about eight years old missing from last night in these woods. I don't know yet what actually happened to him, but he's missing. Spread out and look for clues, a jacket or something that may help. If you find the boy, yell. Now spread out."

Everyone took a different direction into the woods. It was pretty dense in this area, other than a couple clearings that were cleaned out for parties by teenagers from the town.

Dave stayed with Alex. "How's your home life? Other than your mother leaving you and your brother alone."

Alex was quiet for a moment and then said, "I wish my brother and I could go live with someone else. Mom isn't the best mom." He went silent.

"Maybe I can have a talk with her and see if she can get a little better at taking care of you two," Dave offered.

Fatal Abductions

"You do that and she'll just punish me. She blames me for everything. She even blamed me for Dad going to prison. Hell, I didn't kill that guy in the bar, my old man did. He was stupid and got caught."

"Okay, I'll see what can be done," Dave said and turned when he heard someone yell. He yelled back and went towards the sound.

Dave and Alex came to one of the volunteers standing by a tree and looking down.

"Whatcha got, Elmer?" he asked the man.

Elmer pointed down to a shoe the size of a child's shoe.

Alex came up and cried, "That's Jeffrey's shoe. He wrote on the sides with his magic markers."

Dave bent down to the shoe and studied it for a moment before picking it up. The laces were untied. It could have slipped off.

"Alex, would there be any person who would want to hurt Jeffrey?" Dave asked.

"No, man, everyone liked Jeff, he was the good son."

Dave went to the boy and said, "Don't put yourself down. I'm sure you are just as good as your brother."

Alex didn't say anything. Dave took a large baggie from his jacket pocket and put the shoe in it. He handed it to Mike who came up. "Take care of this. It's the boy's shoe."

Mike took it and held on to it. Dave thanked Elmer and took Alex to the nearest clearing. They stood looking around, seeing nothing out of the ordinary.

"I've got no idea why your brother was taken or what the light had to do with it. This area is usually a place for teens to hang out. Do you think maybe someone is after a few young people?"

"Are you asking me?" Alex said.

"Why not? You have a brain. Put it to good use other than getting into mischief."

"I do know there are a lot of us who hang out here, but why would someone want to take anyone?"

"Lots of reasons, child trafficking for one."

"Huh?" Alex uttered.

"There are bad men who grab kids and put them into slavery. Mostly out of the country."

"That's sick, man. What kind of people would do that?"

"As I said, bad men."

They heard another yell from one of the volunteers. They ran towards the sound and came out to a meadow just past the woods, by the road.

Fatal Abductions

"What do you have, Frank?" Dave asked the man standing, looking out to the field of tall weeds and pointing.

Dave looked over and saw it. A very large, round indent in the weeds. It reminded him of the crop circles he had seen on TV. They went to the center of the flattened land and looked around.

"Dave, this is one of those saucer prints in the weeds. This is not normal for this area."

"Frank, don't start anything we can't answer. We have a flattened out area that could have been caused by kids pulling a prank."

"Yeah, but it coincides with the missing kid. How do you explain that? The light, the missing kid and this. Don't tell me you don't think it could be an alien abduction."

"Frank, you're one of the few people I know who believes in aliens. Don't go starting rumors now, please."

Frank stood looking at Dave. "You' re thinking this could be an abduction, aren't you?"

"Yes, but not by aliens. I think I have to call the FBI in on this," Dave said, thinking about his friend, Warren Stevens.

*

Chapter 3

The men continued the search for another hour. They found nothing more to give a hint as to what happened to the boy. They all met back at the cars and stood looking disappointed.

"Let's not fret about this. There's a reason for Jeff's disappearance, and we'll figure it out. I'm calling this an abduction, but not by aliens," he said, looking at Frank. "So don't go talking like that. Now I'm going to call the FBI since they handle kidnappings. Especially of children. I want to thank each of you for helping. Now go home or wherever and we'll call you if we need you again," Dave said.

The men went to their cars and drove out.

Mike and Virgil stood by the patrol car as Dave said, "Guys, go back to the office and I'll be there shortly." The two men got into the car and left.

Dave went to Alex standing by the side of the road looking out to the woods.

"I didn't want anything to happen to the kid. He was my brother and I cared for him, really," Alex said. "If I had known this would happen, we wouldn't have been in the woods."

Fatal Abductions

"Alex, you can't blame yourself. It was something that happened and you couldn't control it. Do you think maybe your brother ran off when the light hit him? You just didn't see him go?"

"If that's what happened, then why didn't I find him last night? I yelled for him until I was hoarse. Your men couldn't find him. I'm sure he couldn't have gone that far."

Dave could see that Alex was tearing up. "Let's go back to the office. We've done as much as we could here. I need to call a friend in the FBI and see if they can help us."

Dave put his hand on the boy's shoulder and pulled him from the side of the road. They got in Dave's Bronco and headed back to the station.

Riding in the car, Dave asked Alex, "Do you want to go home to see if Jeff returns?"

"Do I have to? I mean I'd like to see Jeff come back, but I don't really want to listen to my mother piss and moan about how I lost him. Somewhere else you can take me?"

Dave thought for a moment and then said, "If you don't mind hanging around the sheriff's office while I call the FBI. It will take a couple hours for them to get over here from Seattle. That would keep you away from home for a while. You can help by telling your story to the Feds."

"Real FBI agents? Wow, I've only seen them on TV, not real ones," Alex said, looking excited.

"I guess that's a vote for hanging around the station. I'll call your mom and let her know you'll be with me for a while."

"Thanks. I won't get in the way."

"We do have a jail cell in the station, if you do get in the way," Dave said, smiling.

Alex went silent then laughed quietly.

They arrived at the building and parked. At the counter Dave called to Mike, who was not at his desk and neither was Virgil.

Mike came out of the conference room and grinned. "Virg and I were just talking."

"Is that why you have powdered sugar on your chin?" Dave asked, trying not to grin. "Get Alex one of those donuts, please."

Mike went back into the conference room that also served as a lunchroom. He came out shortly after with a napkin holding a donut. He handed it to Alex then went to his desk.

Virgil came out wiping his mouth with a napkin. He went to his desk also.

Mike said, "I called Warren Stevens about the case and he said he'd be right over, as soon as Walt gets the van gassed up."

Fatal Abductions

"Very good, Mike. I appreciate the call." He turned to Alex and said, "You can go sit in the conference room or at the chair next to my desk until the Feds get here. Your choice."

"I'd like to watch you guys work, if that's okay," he said.

"Work? We don't do much work here in the station," Virgil said. "Dave, I think I'll go out on patrol."

"Good idea. Take Alex with you. He may enjoy watching you give out tickets to speeders," Dave said as he sat at his desk. "I'll call you when Warren gets here."

"Come on, Alex. Now you'll see how we really work around here." He stood and took the boy out to the patrol car.

"Think Alex is telling the truth about his brother?" Mike asked Dave.

"It's a stretch on the light thing, but there's a child missing and we need to find him. I don't believe in flying saucers, but if he's telling the truth, then there's some reason for the light."

"I can't say I believe in aliens, but I haven't seen proof there is life besides us."

"A lot of the people living around here will say if it isn't in the Bible, then it doesn't exist. There are things out there that just haven't been explained or discovered. I'm sure everyone will write this off as a runaway kid. Especially with an absent mother," Dave said.

Bob Moats

"Are you going to talk to CPS about her?"

"I'm not fond of Child Protective Services, but if it keeps the boys safe, then it has to be done."

"I know Agnes has a boyfriend. He's a nasty piece of work. Dan Dillon."

"Dirty Danny? That's who she's been seeing? What the hell would she see in him?" Dave asked.

"He's a bad boy, just like her husband. If Jake knew his wife was fooling around while he was in prison, he'd have a fit," Mike said with a grin.

"I'd rather see Dan in prison. Jake was an idiot but he wasn't really a bad person. He just got the bad breaks. I hope his boys get a better life."

"I went to school with Jake. He was a pistol. Alex looks a lot like him," Mike said.

"I just hope he doesn't act like his dad. Alex seems like he's smart. He just needs to use his brain for better things than getting in trouble."

"Maybe you could hire him to watch the office while we're out."

"Maybe not a bad idea. Just to answer the phones and do a little filing. I'll wait and see how this turns out and have a talk with him."

About an hour later, Warren Stevens and his sidekick, Walt Meyers, came into the station.

Fatal Abductions

"I see you flew over here. How do you keep from getting a ticket for speeding?" Dave asked his friend.

"Most of the cops recognize the van. It just screams federal property," he said with a laugh. "What's the story?"

"Got a kid went missing last night. His brother said it was from a bright light shining down from above. It looks like a case of alien abduction, but since I don't think it was, we have a kidnapping of some kind," Dave said as he went to the counter to shake his friend's hand.

"He said it was a light from above? And you don't believe him?" Walt asked.

Dave looked at the young agent. "You believe in alien abductions, Walt?"

"No, but we've had a number of sightings in the greater Seattle area. Strange lights skimming the ground and people vanishing. At least that's the reports we have," Walt replied.

"Nothing came of our investigations. The missing people just vanished. No clues or forensics to go on. Like they were just pulled up off the ground and taken away," Warren said.

"Now you're trying to scare me aren't you?" Dave said.

"Nope, facts. We've had three disappearances in the last week. Seems the source of the abductions has moved over to here," Warren said.

"Great. Now I have to deal with aliens. It was bad enough with the terrorist and the serial killers. Now Sarah is going to be carrying her gun again."

"Speaking of my girlfriend, how is she?" Warren laughed.

"Still off limits to you. She's doing better after her forced abduction to Las Vegas. We did good on that, didn't we?"

"Yep, and Walt did good at the casino. I'm still trying to figure out how he could win all that loot," Warren said as he looked at Walt.

"I keep telling you, it was just dumb luck," Walt pleaded.

"Okay, you stick to that story." He turned back to Dave. "Now, where is this kid who saw this light?"

"He's out on patrol with Virgil. I'll call and have them come back." Dave went to the radio and called for Virgil. Virgil answered and said he was already on the way back.

About five minutes later Virgil and Alex came into the station. "That was so cool!" Alex said as they came to the counter.

"Alex, this is Special Agent Warren Stevens and his partner Walt Meyers."

Warren held out his hand and Alex shook it. "You got ID?" Alex asked.

Fatal Abductions

Warren was a little surprised and took out his badge wallet and showed the boy. "Not that I didn't believe the sheriff. I just wanted to see the ID. Cool," Alex said.

Everyone laughed. Warren said, "Does it meet with your approval, Alex?"

"Sure does. Just like they show on TV," he said.

"Same thing. Now can we talk about this light you saw last night?"

"I suppose you aren't going to believe me either," Alex said.

Walt said, "Actually, we will believe you. You aren't the first to see it."

*

Chapter 4

"Seriously? Others have seen the light too?" Alex said, sounding relieved he wasn't the only one.

"Seriously. Now tell me all about last night," Warren said.

"Let's go in the conference room where we can sit," Dave said. They all went in except Mike who stayed at his desk. They took chairs and sat.

"Start from the beginning," Warren asked.

Alex repeated the story once again as everyone listened. He finished and waited for a response.

"It seems to fit the other reports," Walt said to Warren.

"Yes, it does." Warren looked at Dave and said, "The three abductions this last week all had the same response from witnesses. A light came down from the sky and nearly blinded everyone. Then when the light went away the person standing below the light was gone."

"I knew I wasn't crazy," Alex said mostly to himself.

"No, Alex, something is going on. We need to go out to the area where this happened to look it over," Warren said to the boy.

"We pretty much covered the area, but maybe fresh eyes will see something we missed," Dave said.

They stood and Dave told Walt to follow him in the van. "Virgil, for the heck of it, go into town and see if anyone else may have seen the light."

Virgil went out as the rest of the men and the boy went out to the cars. "It's not far, just stay behind me."

Fatal Abductions

"Only if you don't drive like an old lady," Warren yelled.

"I, at least, do the speed limit," Dave yelled back.

They drove back to the Forestry service road and parked. Dave told Alex to take the lead. He went into the woods followed by everyone else.

Dave said to Warren, "I forgot to mention, we found one of the boy's shoes. Mike has it."

"I'll have Walt look at it when we get back. Damn, I hate going into woods. Bugs, bears and swamps," Warren said.

"We only have bugs and bears. No swamps." Dave laughed.

"What if we meet a bear?" Walt asked.

Warren grinned and said, "You'll just have to run faster than I do."

Alex stopped and said they were there. Warren asked him to go through the motions of what happened.

"I was hiding behind that tree when the light came down and lit up the spot where Jeff was standing. It blinded me for a couple seconds then it went out. Jeff was gone."

Walt had a boxy device and turned it on. The box clicked softly.

"What's that?" Alex asked.

"It detects radiation. It will tell us if there's any sign of radioactive residue left by the light."

"Wow, you think it could be dangerous?" Alex asked.

"There's not enough of it to hurt us. But there seems to be a little radiation in this area," Walt replied.

Dave said, "I heard that years ago there was some attempt to mine uranium in this area. But they didn't find enough to make it worthwhile. That may be what you are finding with that thing."

Walt looked disappointed and shut the device off. Warren was looking up at the treetops. "It looks like the top most points were cut off. What do you think?"

"I noticed that earlier. Almost as if they were trimmed," Dave said.

"I wish we had the chopper, to look at the area from above."

"Or one of those jet packs so you could fly up," Alex said.

"Yeah, that would be nice too. But we don't have any jet packs in our arsenal of toys," Warren said to the boy. "Now which way did you search last night?"

Alex looked around and pointed. "I first went that way. I don't know why but I did."

Fatal Abductions

"Nothing was over there?" Warren asked.

"No. I yelled for my brother, but he didn't answer."

"Where did you find the shoe?" he asked Dave.

"One of our searchers found it over here." He started to walk that way and they came to the area. "Right here. The shoelaces were undone, so it may have slipped off his foot."

Walt was looking around and spotted something in the tall grass. He put on rubber gloves and picked up the object. He brought it to Warren and showed it to him.

"It's an air cartridge. The kind they use in paint guns." He looked at Dave and continued, "You get any of those around here, kids playing shoot-em-up?"

"Not that I've seen. But who knows what these kids do out here?" Dave said. He looked at Alex and asked, "Have you seen anyone with paint guns out here?"

"No, but that can be used in a pellet gun too. Some guys come out here to pick off crows."

"True, it would fit a large pellet gun. Bag it, Walt. Maybe we can get some prints off it. Worth looking at."

Virgil was standing by the men and said, "That could also be used in a tranquilizer gun. The vet in town had one when he went out to tranquilize a wounded deer a couple months back."

Warren smiled and said, "Or to shoot a kid."

They dug around the area a while longer then decided to call it as it was starting to get dark.

"Let's go back to the office and talk," Dave said. "Alex, would you like to stay the night with us at my house?"

Alex's eyes got big and he said, "Wow, sure. That would be great."

"He gets the sleeping bag on the floor," Warren said quickly. "I get the couch. Walt can sleep in the van."

"You have this all planned out, don't you?" Dave said.

"Got to be ready for any situation. Motto of the FBI."

"I thought it was 'We get our man' or something like that," Virgil said.

"That's the Canadian Mounties. They know how to get it done," Warren said.

"Whatever, let's get out of the woods before we attract a bear," Dave said. Warren turned and headed back to the cars quickly.

As they were walking back to the cars, Alex said quietly to Dave, "You do know there aren't any bears in this area?"

"I know, but Warren doesn't. It makes him move faster," he said with a laugh.

Fatal Abductions

They got back to the station and Mike was at the counter. "Dave, Agnes called and said Jeff hadn't come back yet. She wanted to know if we found anything. I told her you'd call when you got back."

"Good, I need to talk to her." He went to his desk and asked Alex for his phone number. Alex told him as Dave was pushing the buttons on the phone.

"Agnes," he said when the woman came on. "Sheriff Chandler here. I wish I could say we have good news, but we haven't located the boy yet. I have the FBI here to help and I'm keeping Alex with me for the night in case I need to have him help in finding Jeffrey." He listened then said, "Good, I'll call in the morning. Stay at the house, just in case I need you." He listened again and then hung up.

"Well, we're set for the night. Let's pack it in and go see if we can surprise Sarah," Dave said.

"She doesn't know about this?" Warren asked.

"It happened after I got in to work this morning and I haven't talked to her since this happened."

"This will be a nice surprise. Are you going to call her and warn her that she's going to have a full house?"

"Nope, I like to shake her up every now and then. Besides, I'll let Walt fill her head with stories about alien abductions," Dave said with a grin.

They went out to the cars after Dave told Virgil to take the midnight shift. He grumbled about it but agreed. Mike said he was going home.

Alex went with Dave as Walt and Warren followed in the van.

"Do you think this is aliens grabbing people?" Alex asked as they drove out to the house.

"What do you think, Alex? Four people have been taken now. Your brother is one of them. Do you think this was aliens?"

"I'm not really believing it was, but what could it be?"

"Use your imagination. Make up a story that could have happened to those people. Be outrageous and daring in your thoughts. Work it out in your head then let me know what you came up with. It's the Occam's Razor principle."

"The who principle?"

"Occam's Razor. It's basically when you have two competing theories that make exactly the same predictions, the simpler one is the better. You know what you saw and it looked like an alien abduction. Now make up another story as to how it could have happened. Compare the two and decide which is simpler. Occam's Razor basically says, keep it simple. Shakespeare once said *'There are more things in heaven and earth, Horatio, than are dreamt of in your philosophy.'*"

"You talk funny." Alex laughed. "But I guess I see what you're getting at. Okay, I'll make up a story in my head as to what may have happened."

"Good. Work on it, put in lots of details and then tell me what you came up with." They arrived at the house and Dave said, "This should be interesting."

They parked and went to the front door. Warren said, "Hold on. Let me go in first." Dave unlocked the door quietly and let Warren go in. They stood in the vestibule listening for where Sarah might be. Warren knew the layout of the house from being there many times before. He could hear Sarah in the living room, at her computer, typing.

Warren slammed the front door and said, "Honey, I'm home." He was standing by the opening to the living room when Sarah came flying around the corner and latched on to him with a big kiss.

Her eyes went wide as she realized it wasn't Dave. She screamed and hit Warren in the gut.

*

Chapter 5

"What the hell?" Warren wailed. "Didn't you recognize me?"

"In the dark of the vestibule? Do you think I can see in the dark?" she replied.

"Then how did you know it wasn't Dave?"

"He's a better kisser," she said with a smile.

"You knew it wasn't Dave before you kissed me, didn't you?" Warren said.

"I saw you guys coming up from the cars. I do pay attention to what goes on around the house. And Van Gogh was whining when you pulled in."

"Smart dog," Dave said, came to his wife and kissed her.

"That's better. Now why's Warren here and what's going on?" she asked Dave.

"It's a long story. I'll fill you in shortly. First, this is Alex, he'll be staying overnight. His younger brother went missing last night in the woods."

"Oh, I'm so sorry, Alex." She went to him and gave him a hug. Dave thought he saw a smile on Alex's face.

"Okay, we need to get in and relax," Dave said, separating Sarah from Alex. "Let's go in the living room and sit." He went that way as everyone followed.

"Can I get anyone refreshments?" Sarah asked.

All the men gave their selections and Sarah went off to the kitchen. Dave pointed Alex to an easy chair and told him to sit there. Alex sat.

"So, Walt, what's your honest opinion as to the abductions?" Dave asked the young agent.

Fatal Abductions

Walt looked uncomfortable and said, "I do believe in life other than on our planet. Think about how many different species of life there are on the earth. We can't survive underwater without air, so how can we say that fish and other underwater creatures are the same as us? They need water to exist. Even though they extract oxygen from the water, they would die if left on land. So why do we assume that a planet that has more sulfur than oxygen can't support life? Maybe these creatures that come here from afar would die in our atmosphere."

"So you think this could be an alien abduction?" asked Alex.

"Alex, I can't explain it without facts. And we need to investigate until we have facts. Your brother disappeared and you couldn't find him although you searched. So where do you think he went to?" Walt said.

Alex was silent. Then he said, "I'm thinking something had to be up in the air. It took my brother, but does it have to be aliens? I mean, it could be some bad earth men who want to steal people for something bad."

Dave grinned. The boy was thinking.

Walt smiled and said, "That's the simple answer for something we feel may be an improbability. Aliens have been reported to have abducted people for years, but there has been no proof other than the statements from those abducted. You're right, it could be earthlings taking people. In this situation, I think that is the real answer."

Alex gave Walt a big smile and then Dave's phone rang. He answered.

"Yeah, Virgil, what is it?" He listened and then hung up. He looked concerned then turned to Warren sitting next to him. "We got another missing person. Taken by a bright light." He stood and said, "Let's go. Alex, you stay here and relax. My wife will bore you to death talking, but it will be safer."

Sarah had come back into the room with a tray of drinks and gave Dave a surprised look. "Now where are you going?"

"Crime doesn't wait." He kissed her and then said, "Have Alex explain everything to you. We have to go." Dave led Warren and Walt out to the cars.

At his Bronco, Dave said to Warren at the van, "I hope this isn't the start of something bad."

"Bad as in people missing?"

"Yeah," he said and got in the car.

They drove to the station and parked. In the station they found a very distraught woman sitting on Mike's chair.

"Dave, you know Virginia Davenport. Her husband, George, disappeared tonight."

Dave went to the woman and said, "Virginia, tell me what happened. Oh, this is Special Agent Warren Stevens and his partner Walt Meyers of the FBI. They are here because of another abduction last night."

Fatal Abductions

"Abduction? Is that what happened to George?" she asked.

"Well, you tell me where George went to."

"I don't know where he went to. That's what you're supposed to find out," she said indignantly.

"I'm sorry, Virginia, I'll rephrase the question. What happened tonight when George disappeared?"

"The light took him," she said.

"Okay, what light?" Dave asked.

"George went out back of the house because the horses were making a racket. We have three that belong to our daughter. They are in the stable and they were making loud noises. Our daughter is away in Seattle visiting a cousin. So George had to go out and see what the ruckus was about." She paused and took a breath. "I was at the back door watching him and as he got to the barn, this bright light came from above and then I couldn't see him. It was very bright. Then the light stopped and he was gone. I ran out and called for him but he wasn't anywhere around. Where did he go, Dave?"

"Virginia, I don't know, but we'll see what we can find out. Can you go to a friend's house for tonight?"

"I have a friend who would let me stay with her, yes."

"I'll have Virgil follow you in your car, while we go to your farm and see what we can find out," Dave said and looked at Warren.

Bob Moats

"Thank you, Dave," she said as she started to tear up. Virgil handed her a tissue from a box on his desk.

"Virgil, get her to where ever she needs to go and come back here," Dave said.

Virgil agreed and took the woman out.

"We can go out, but it's dark and I don't think we'll find much tonight. Think we should bother to go out tonight?" Dave said.

"While it's fresh, sure. I'm not fond of wandering around a farm, but we should at least look. Maybe the aliens are still hovering over." Warren smiled. "A question? Why did she come here and not just call?"

"George had a battle with the phone company, fees too high, so he canceled his service. He had a cell phone, but I presume it disappeared with him. Shall we go then?"

They went out to the cars and Dave said, "I'll go with you in the van. No sense in taking my car."

They drove out as Dave gave directions to the farm. It was out in the country, about four miles from the town. They pulled into the drive and then up to the barn.

Walt parked and they got out. The horses were still making noises and they went to the open barn door. "They must be upset about something," Walt said.

Dave went in and flipped on a light switch on the side of door. The barn interior lit and he could see three horses in stalls acting agitated.

39

Fatal Abductions

"I don't know much about horses, but something is wrong with them," Warren said.

"Maybe it's the aliens," Dave said with a smile. They went back out to the yard to where Walt was standing looking around.

"You were right, Dave, it's very dark out here," Walt said.

"Hold on," Dave said, went to a box on the outside of the barn, opened it and flipped a switch. The yard lit up from three quartz lamps. "Is that better?" Dave smiled.

"The woman said she saw her husband from the back door of the house." Warren turned to the door and walked to it. He stepped up on the porch and looked out to the yard. "It's a clear view from here. Walt, see if you can find any prints on the ground."

Walt had already been looking as soon as the lights went on. He was walking around the front of the barn. "There's foot prints coming from the house to the barn, but there's so many it's hard to tell whose is whose. Plus we walked all over the area. Not very good investigating," Walt said with a grin.

Warren went to Walt and looked at the ground also. "Yep, bad move. But I don't see any alien twelve toe prints. So where did he go?"

"I can't read the ground, it's a mess. But there does look to be a bit of a scuffle over here. Could be when the man was grabbed. Hard to tell who may have been involved in the scuffle, but the prints look human. No twelve toed prints," Walt said to Dave.

Dave laughed and then went to the edge of the lights perimeter. He stepped out into the dark and looked around. Walt and Warren joined him.

"See anything?" Warren asked.

"Just a million stars in the sky. One thing I like about the country, it's dark and the stars have a chance of being seen better. I used to go out to a big field by my parents' house, spread out a blanket, lie down and watch the stars. Then think about traveling in a rocket going way out into deep space," Dave said.

"Yeah, you are a space cadet. If I had the money, I'd put you on a rocket ship to the stars." Warren laughed.

Walt made a noise then pointed to an area of the sky just above the horizon. It was hard to tell how far, but there was something large in the sky. It blocked out the stars making a black hole in the sky. And it was moving.

*

Chapter 6

"Damn. What could it be?" Warren said.

"Well, it's not a plane, moving too slow," Dave said. "And it's big."

"It's a saucer," Walt said.

"Are you going to start that now?" Warren asked his partner.

"No, I mean the shape is a saucer. Not a space saucer. It's heading out to the north. What's up there, Dave?"

"Mountains. Mostly big mountains. If it keeps going, it will be over water then into Canada. Maybe the Canadians are kidnapping our people for experimentation," Dave said, trying not to laugh.

"You are just so funny," Warren said as they watched the dark object moving away.

"Shall I call air command?" Walt asked.

"By the time they rousted, it will be gone," Warren replied.

"Good, maybe it's going away," Dave said.

"Sure, but it has two of your people. You need to get them back. I'm calling for a chopper to get out here in case we have this visitor again," Warren said. "I want to chase that thing."

They stood watching it go off into the distance, flying out over uninhabited lands.

"So now we got a missing man and a mysterious object in the sky. Can you call the Air Force and see if they have some sort of secret aircraft that flies like that?" Dave asked his friend. "Or has it on radar?"

"Good idea, now that we know there's something up there. Walt, go into the van and see if you can get the nearest base. Ask if they got a blip on their radar."

Walt went to the van and disappeared into it. Dave turned back to the barn. "Listen, the horses are quiet now. That thing has gone and they know it."

"Animals can sense disasters. Like earthquakes. It bothers their senses. Maybe the horses could feel the aircraft coming," Warren said.

"Makes sense to me," Dave replied as they watched the black hole get smaller until it vanished. "Why the hell did they take these people?"

"We'll find out when we track them down."

A few minutes later Walt came back. "Sea-Tac airport and Bangor Trident Base didn't report any sightings of aircraft out here. Their radar goes a long way. But that only explains that the thing is flying low, well below radar. They also said nothing unidentified came through their airspace."

Fatal Abductions

"Okay, it's big, dark, flies slow and low. What does that sound like?" Dave asked.

"Beats me," Warren said. "I'll call Nellis air base in Nevada and see if they have something like that."

"Call Area 51 also. See if they lost a flying saucer," Dave said with a smirk.

"You are just a regular comic," Warren said. "I don't see anything more to do out here. Let's go back and open that beer Sarah was bringing out."

"Yeah, before her and Alex finish it off." Dave laughed.

Dave shut off all the outside lights and they went to the van and drove back to the house.

Sarah was at the door waiting for them. "Did you catch the saucer people?" she asked as the men came up on the porch.

"Funny. I hope Alex didn't fill your head with wild stories."

"No, he was rational. I filled in the details myself. I have seen enough sci-fi movies to know all about alien invasions," she said excitedly.

"This is not an invasion," Dave said as he pushed Sarah back into the house. "There were no death rays or buildings blowing up. Just one unidentified object in the sky and two missing people."

44

"Two missing? So my brother isn't the only one?" Alex said as he came to them.

"No, Alex. A man was taken tonight. His wife said it was a bright light. So we now know you were right," Warren said.

"Good, I thought I was going crazy. No, not good because a man disappeared, just good that I was right."

"We got it, Alex. Now where is that beer you had?" Dave said to Sarah.

"We drank it all," she said with a grin.

"I doubt you drank the whole case I bought." He went past her to the kitchen and took three beers out of the fridge. He gave one to Warren and one to Walt. They all went into the living room again.

"I hope there are no more abductions tonight," Dave said.

"I think that thing moved out of the area for now," Walt said. "But it only strikes at night. So be prepared."

"I'm calling the bureau in Seattle and get a chopper out here." He stood and went out to the vestibule to make a call.

"I heard Mr. Meyers say that thing moved away. Did you see the thing?" Alex asked.

Fatal Abductions

"We saw what appeared to be an object in the sky blocking out the stars. It was big and moved slowly. But we don't know what it could be for now," Dave said.

"Big and slow? Sounds like a flying saucer to me," Sarah said.

"You watch too many movies," Dave said to her.

"How else would I know to protect us from an invasion? We need someone with a severe cold to give them germs," she said.

"That's from 'The War of the Worlds,' written by H.G. Wells," Dave said.

"No, I'm referring to 'First Men in the Moon,' by H.G. Wells. Was he obsessed with aliens?"

"I guess so. Either way germs stopped the aliens. Now can we talk about anything else but aliens?" Dave said.

"How about the zombies that invaded the town?" Alex asked.

Dave groaned and said, "Can we not talk about that either."

Warren came back in and said, "Got a chopper coming in the morning and a pilot at our disposal. You have enough room in your front yard to land the bird, don't you? I told them to get a fix on the GPS from the van."

"You're going to have a helicopter land here?" Sarah asked.

"Yep, in the morning."

"That is so cool. Can we take a ride in it?" Alex asked.

"I don't think the pilot will appreciate giving joy rides. But I'll see," Warren said with a smile.

They sat for a while trying to talk about anything other than aliens and zombies. It wasn't easy but they managed. Finally Dave said he was tired and wanted to go to bed.

"I get the couch," Warren said.

"Alex can have the guest room," Sarah said.

"I thought the guest room was filled with your packing boxes," Warren said.

"We put the ones not needed in a storage unit, and I fixed it up for guests. But since you were so nice to call for the couch, Alex can have the guest room."

Warren was speechless. He couldn't kick the kid out of the guest room now, so he didn't say anything.

"I'll sleep in the van," Walt said. "Just in case a call comes in over the system. Alex, tomorrow I'll show you the van. It has all kinds of electronic gear."

"Yeah, I'd like that," the boy replied.

Fatal Abductions

Everyone went off to their respective places to sleep. About an hour later when everyone was passed out, a bright light shone down in the back yard. Van Gogh was bouncing around in the living room at the huge windows. Warren stirred and told the dog to go to bed. The light moved away before Warren saw it.

The next morning there was a horrible noise outside and Dave came flying out of the bedroom. "What the hell is that?" he yelled to Warren, who was just getting up.

"It's the chopper. They must have left early." Warren was dressed since he hadn't undressed to sleep on the couch. He went to the front door and opened it, going out. Alex came running up behind him to see the chopper landing on the huge front lawn.

"Oh wow. So cool," he said from the porch. Shortly everyone came out to greet the pilot. Walt came out of the van and over to the others.

"Agent Harris reporting," the pilot said to Warren as he came up.

"Welcome, Harris," Warren said as he introduced everyone. Alex was walking around the chopper checking it out. "That young man is Alex. He's our witness to an abduction from an unknown aircraft that takes people in a beam of bright light."

"Like the three from the Seattle area?" Harris asked.

"Then you do know about it?"

"I had to fly around looking for the thing the other day, found nothing."

"Well, we sort of saw it last night. But just a void in the stars. Big and slow. Like a chopper, but no noise."

"Stealth chopper?" the pilot asked.

"That's a possibility, but it would have to be reported to fly in this area," Warren said.

"Not if it belongs to a drug cartel. I've heard they got hold of one about six months ago. But they were down in Mexico. Can't see them flying all the way up here without being seen or refueling."

"Maybe the Canadians have one?" Dave asked.

"I haven't heard if they do. But they don't share much with us," Harris said.

"Well, it's good to have you around. Why don't you take a fly around to check out the area? Get the lay of the land," Warren said, then looked at Alex. "Maybe you could take our young witness to see if he sees anything."

Alex looked shocked and said, "Wow! I'd like that."

Harris said, "Okay, let's fly." He took the boy and instructed him what to do while in flight.

After they were ready, the pilot took off, blowing everything in the yard around. Everyone ran to the house as the huge beast lifted off.

"I'm sure Alex won't forget this day too soon," Sarah said.

*

Chapter 7

The chopper was gone for about thirty minutes then returned. Everyone came out to greet Alex and the pilot. The pilot told Warren he got a good look at the terrain.

"Holy crap, that was really great!" Alex said as he got out.

"I talked to your mother while you were gone. Jeff still hasn't come back and I told her you were going to stay with us for a few days until we solve this," Dave said.

"I'd like that. I can help with anything you need," Alex said.

"Oh, you'll earn your room and board," Sarah said with a smile.

"Shall we all go get something to eat? It's almost lunch time," Dave said.

"Let's go to the Halfway House for burgers," Sarah said.

"Sounds good," Dave replied. They all went to get into Dave's car and drive into town to the restaurant. Walt wanted to drive the van in case something came up. Alex asked if he could go with Walt. Dave let him.

On the way Alex said to Walt, "This is some van. Looks like you have lots of good things."

Walt smiled and said, "It contains all the latest electronic devices. Listening, snooping, and tracking, well…everything to do our job. Within the law and slightly outside occasionally."

"A real spy mobile, huh?"

"I guess you could say that. We do spy but for the right reasons. To stop bad people from breaking laws or hurting others."

"Can anyone be an FBI agent?"

"It's a process to join the feds. From what I've seen, you could be an agent when you're older. If you wanted to be. It's not all fun, and not like you see on TV. We investigate crimes and sometimes it's boring work. Other times it's very rewarding, like when you save people who have been kidnapped. But we don't always succeed."

"You're thinking of my brother?"

"I don't want to get your hopes up, but we may not be able to find him. It's best to be prepared for it. That's one thing they don't tell you in FBI training, the sadness when a case goes bad. You need to harden up for those days."

Fatal Abductions

Alex was quiet on the rest of the drive. Walt let him have his thoughts.

They pulled into the parking for the restaurant. Everyone got out and went into the building.

Warren whispered into Dave's ear, "Is your daughter here?"

"Warren you're a douche," Dave replied.

Sarah was behind them and laughed. "Dave has children all over town," she said to Warren.

"I do not. Cut it out," Dave protested. "Warren, you crack a joke or say anything to Clara, I swear I'll shoot you under the table, right where it counts."

Warren shut up, but laughed. They went to a table and sat. Clara came bouncing up and passed out menus. "Hey, Dave, Sarah. Who's your friends?"

Dave introduced everyone. Clara said, "I already know Alex. We go to school together. Is he under arrest?"

Dave said, "No, his brother is missing and he's helping us to find him."

Clara had a surprised look, "Oh, I'm sorry, Alex. I didn't know. I hope you find him."

"It's okay, Clara. Thanks."

Warren started to talk. Dave interrupted him. "Don't need to talk Warren. Just order."

Bob Moats

"That's what I was going to do," he said with a grin. He gave his order as everyone else did. Clara went off to place the order and get their drinks.

"Dave, Alex is thinking of maybe joining the FBI. Think he could handle it? You know him," Walt said.

Dave looked at Alex and smiled. "I think he'd be a good agent. He's got street smarts. Better than some agents I know," he said, looking at Warren.

"Hey, I got street smarts. I use them all the time," Warren defended himself.

"No comment," was all Dave said and took a sip of his drink that Clara brought to the table.

They ate their meals and finished. Then they paid and left a big tip for Clara. As they were leaving, Warren said quietly to Dave, "I think she looks like you." He hit Warren in the stomach with the back of his hand.

They got into the car and Dave said, "I think we should go to George's farm again and look while it's light."

"I'm for that," Sarah said. "About time I got involved."

"I could drop you off at home," Dave joked.

"Not getting rid of me that easily. Now drive, lackey."

"Her vocabulary is getting better." Warren laughed.

53

Fatal Abductions

"Shut up," Dave warned him.

They arrived at the farm. Virginia wasn't home. Dave said she probably was still at her friend's house. They went around the back yard looking around. Alex hung close to Sarah.

"It looks no better in the light than it did last night. I'm wondering what is in the direction of the flight path for the thing?" Warren said and pulled his cell phone. He called the pilot and said to come get him at the GPS location of the van. He told him there was plenty of room to land.

"Are you going alone?" Walt asked.

"Yep, I want to see what there is from the air."

"There's just mountains up there, but if it will make you happy, go for it," Dave said.

"I will."

About ten minutes later the chopper arrived and took Warren up. He waved as they sailed away in the direction the saucer took.

"I think he just wanted to take a ride," Walt said. "He loves flying in the helicopter."

"Well, if it gets him out of our hair, all the better," Dave said with a grin to the younger agent.

They looked around the farm yard a while longer, finding nothing.

"If George was taken by the light, there would be no evidence. Just a last pair of footprints before he went up," Sarah said. "Too bad. George was a nice man."

"Don't say was, dear. We'll find him. He still is a nice man," Dave told her. "Walt, call Warren and tell him we're heading back to the house."

Walt called the senior agent and relayed the message. Everyone got back in the car and Dave drove back.

When they arrived, the chopper was already there. Warren and the pilot were sitting on the porch, waiting.

"You took long enough." Warren laughed.

"Fine, flyboy. What did you see?" Dave asked.

"Nothing. Nothing at all. No flying saucer or anything that would hint of a saucer going to or landing in the mountains. Unless the thing went underground, it was nowhere to be seen. Find anything else at the farm?"

"Nope, same, nothing. Everything happened above ground, in the air. So there's nothing to see on the ground. Something came down through the light and grabbed the people, taking them up into the flying object. Leaving no trace."

"Okay let's assume that there is a machine that can fly slow and hover. They shine a bright light down to disorient people, then someone or something comes down and latches on to the victim and pulls them up into the machine. The machine flies away and there's no sign of an abduction. Quick and neat. Unless there was a witness, they would get away with it cleanly," Walt said.

"I like your theory. It's the best we have now. So the only way to stop this thing is to confront it in the air?" Dave asked.

"I'm thinking that. We have no trace or evidence. Maybe tonight we put people high up and see if they can spot the light. We wait for the alert and use the chopper to fly out to find out what we are up against," Walt said.

"I can have Virgil and Mike up in the spotting towers for forest fires and watch for the light. They're high enough to see all over the area."

"Sounds like a winner. Set them up and we'll rig radios to communicate with them," Warren said.

Dave called Virgil at the station and asked if Mike was in yet. They both were there. "Stay there, we're coming in."

"We don't know if the thing is even going to do a run tonight, but we'll be prepared." Warren turned to the pilot and said, "It may be a long night so get some rest now. In fact everyone needs to rest before it gets dark."

"I'll agree to that," Dave said. "After I go to the station to talk to the guys, we'll all take a nap, if possible, then get up just before dusk."

"I'll go with you to the station. Walt, get some radios ready to go."

Walt ran out to the van and brought out a pair of radios, handing them to Warren. Dave was in his car and Warren got in. "Go get some rest. It could be a long night," he told Walt. Dave drove off.

"In Seattle they took three people. So far they got two here. I'm thinking they may go for another. Then off to another area to grab some people. Just my opinion," Warren said.

"As good as any."

"I hope they do a run tonight. We are ready for them. Walt has his arsenal of weapons at our disposal. We'll blast them out of the sky." Warren was eager to take down the craft.

"Let's just see where they go. I'd like to get Jeff and George back safely."

"Well, it stands to reason we get them back safe and sound," Warren said with a grin.

"I'm glad you agree. Maybe we can do an exchange with the aliens, you for Jeff and George."

"Nah, they wouldn't want me, I'm too tough to capture."

"Or to eat," Dave said with a smirk.

*

Chapter 8

They arrived at the station and went in to find Mike and Virgil standing in the hallway. They had backpacks on a bench next to them.

"What you got there, guys?" Dave asked.

"Supplies. Snacks, water, portable radio, stuff we'll need out on the towers," Virgil said.

"Fine, just pay attention for any lights. Warren has a couple radios for you to keep in communication with Walt in the van. As soon as you see any strange lights, call and give us the coordinates. You have an idea on what to look for so don't wait to call," Dave said.

"You got it, Dave. We'll get George and Jeff back," Mike said.

Warren handed the walkie-talkies to the men and showed them how to work them. They tested them, hearing Walt answering back.

"To conserve batteries don't turn them on unless you see something," Warren explained.

"If we need to talk to you, we can use our cell phones. The radios are quicker to reach us," Dave said. "Okay, go to the towers and get set up."

The deputies left and Dave said to Warren, "Well, it's going to be a long night, I figure."

"If this object appears tonight, we'll be ready. The pilot can have us in the air in minutes and there's enough radar and other tracking devices on the chopper to find where this thing goes to," Warren said as they walked out the front door. Dave locked it up and they went to the car.

They arrived back at the house and everyone was resting but not sleeping. Sarah heard the men arrive and went to the door followed by Van Gogh. She opened the door as they came up and asked, "Are they ready?"

"They should be in place by now. All we can do is wait to hear from them," Dave said to her as he put his arms around her and pulled her to him. "Let's get some rest. We'll need it if we have to go chasing in the middle of the night."

Warren went to the couch. Walt was in the van with the pilot, resting and waiting for a call. Dave went to the bedroom with Sarah, leaving the door opened to hear anything. Alex was in the guestroom, his door also opened.

"If they do spot the thing, you stay here with Alex. We don't have a lot of room in the chopper for everyone," Dave told Sarah.

"I'm not crazy about flying in an upside down weed whacker. I'm sure you men can take care of the situation. Alex and I will be fine here."

Fatal Abductions

They lay on the bed, both staring at the ceiling. Van Gogh was at the end of the bed between their legs and snorted. That made both Dave and Sarah laugh.

~~*~~

The sun went down and it was now dark. Mike was walking around the perimeter of the north tower normally used to spot forest fires in the area. Budget cuts in the forestry service took the spotters out of the towers. They were mostly unused now except by adventurous persons who risked climbing the tall structures. The two towers were now rusting and maintenance was nearly non-existent. Virgil would call Mike on his cell every so often from the south tower to be sure Mike was still awake.

The area was relatively quiet other than the crickets giving out the temperature by their chirps. Mike was counting the chirps and trying to do the math in his head. He gave up and watched the horizon for signs of a large black void or a bright light anywhere in the sky.

An hour later he was trying not to nod off as he sat in the one chair left in the tower. He was now inside the small building at the top of the tower which was missing most of its windows, broken by vandals. The chair wasn't comfortable but it was available. He was watching out one of the few windows still having glass when he saw something. He stood and got close to the glass. It was hard to see through the dirty pane, so he went out of the room

60

to the railing around the edge. He strained to see what he thought was something moving in the distance.

He pulled the radio clipped to his belt and turned it on, just in case. He watched for a moment then jumped when his cell phone buzzed. He pulled it out of his pocket and looked at the caller ID. It was Virgil.

"What?" he said.

"Did you see that?" Virgil's voice came through the speaker.

"What did you see?"

"I'm not sure, but I think it's big and moving slowly towards you from the north." Virgil's voice came out clearly to Mike since he had the speaker on now.

"Okay, I think I see something. But I haven't seen a light yet."

"I think we should call in anyway. It could be the saucer hunting for a victim."

Mike hesitated and then said, "I'll call." He hung up on Virgil, pushed the talk button on the walkie-talkie and spoke into it. "Walt, come in."

Walt's voice came back, "What is it? Got a sighting?"

"Virgil and I both think we see some object moving around out here. Maybe you should get them up in the air and out here to check it out."

Fatal Abductions

"I'll get them up and flying. Thanks, Mike." Walt clicked off as Mike was watching the void in the stars moving slowly towards town. He was now frightened by the specter. Was this really an alien ship taking people for probing or worse? He hoped it wouldn't come by the tower.

~~*~~

Walt banged on the door of the house and then opened it. "We have a sighting!" he yelled from the vestibule. Warren was already by his side as Dave came running out of the bedroom.

"Is the pilot ready?" Warren asked.

"He's firing up the chopper now. I put as many weapons in as possible without weighing the thing down. I'll listen from the van and have the men report what they see and relay it to you."

"Great," Warren said and then he and Dave ran to the chopper, already warming up.

They got in and Warren put on the headset that was linked to Walt in the van. Walt gave the coordinates to the pilot from where Mike last said they saw the object. The pilot turned on the internal radar and then lifted off.

Dave felt his stomach drop as the chopper shot up into the night. He watched from his seat behind Warren in the front. Warren was studying the gauges on the radar but was not seeing anything.

"Walt, ask the men if they still see it."

A few moments later Walt came back and gave the coordinates to the next sighting. The pilot adjusted his flight and they headed that way.

"I'm still not seeing anything on the radar," Warren said.

"Could they have some kind of shielding that prevents radar from picking them up?" Dave asked.

"I have no idea. This is some machine that travels and can't be seen by my instruments." He said then, "Walt, patch me through to Mike."

"Warren, Mike here," came the voice from the chopper's speakers.

"Do you see us in the air?"

"Yes, I see your lights now. You are about a mile from the object. Head more to the north from where you are. It's still heading towards you," Mike said, sounding a little panicky now.

"Mike, take a breath and watch were we go. Tell us if we are close."

"Will do," Mike came back.

Fatal Abductions

Warren yelled over the chopper noise to Dave, "We need to get a visual on this. My instruments are useless."

"I'll watch the right, you watch the left," Dave yelled back.

The pilot kept heading north towards the unknown object that they hadn't seen yet.

Suddenly the pilot banked the chopper to the left as he nearly came in contact with something ahead.

"Shit, it's right in front of us now," the pilot yelled as he did his best to avoid a collision with the dark object.

He banked back and around to what he believed to be alongside of the craft.

"It's huge!" he yelled.

Warren was trying to aim a spotlight on the thing. "The light doesn't even illuminate it! The light just disappears into the thing."

The pilot was trying to control the chopper now as it was starting to bounce around.

"Watch out!" Warren yelled as he saw what looked like two huge propellers on the top of the thing. The pilot pulled up before he came in contact with the propellers.

"Hell, it's like a giant helicopter," the pilot yelled.

He banked again and tried to keep the chopper from vibrating. "Something is shaking us and if I don't get away from this monster we'll break apart." He pulled up from the object, moving away.

The chopper started to smooth out as Warren and Dave tried to see what they could make of the object.

"I can't see all of it. The thing is too black to gauge a size, but it is big," Warren yelled.

"How the hell do they hide something that size?" Dave asked.

Suddenly a bright light came from the object and blinded everyone on the chopper.

"Get us out of here, it's attacking!" Warren yelled.

The pilot banked again away from the light and went down fast. He skimmed the trees below hoping to find a safe place to land. The spotlight attached under the chopper shone on the ground until they saw a clearing. The pilot put the chopper down as carefully as he could and shut the thing down.

They watched above as they saw the black void pass overhead.

*

Chapter 9

They were out of the chopper now watching the thing overhead. The pilot went to check the rotor blades to be sure they weren't damaged.

Suddenly the light beam hit the pilot. Dave was closest to him and ran, taking a leap into the light to grab the pilot. He was surprised to find two people in the light that he hit. He grabbed on to one person as he moved out of the light. He had the pilot.

Warren was coming around with his weapon drawn, aiming into the light as he saw a dark mass flying up towards the object from the ground. Dave got up and pulled his gun, coming alongside Warren.

"There was someone else in the beam besides Harris," Dave yelled to Warren.

"Well, he's gone now," Warren replied.

The beam of light suddenly shut down and the object moved quickly away leaving the men alone below.

"It moves fast when it wants to," Dave said.

"I guess we frightened it," Warren said with a slight nervous laugh.

They looked over to the pilot. He was lying on the ground, not moving.

"Damn, did they kill him?" Warren said as the men ran to Harris.

Warren checked his pulse and said, "He's alive."

Dave beamed his flashlight at Harris as Warren checked him for any sign of blood. He did find a small projectile sticking from Harris' side.

"It's a tranq dart. They shot him with it to knock him out," he said as he put on gloves to pull the dart out and put it in a bag from his pocket. "At least we have something from them. Now we can see if this is made here on Earth or not."

Dave was looking around and said, "We have a small problem."

"Now what?" Warren said, sounding exasperated.

"With Harris out, can you fly the chopper? Because I can't."

Warren stood. "No, I can't either. We'll just have to wait until he wakes. I'm going to call Walt and let him know we're all right." He went to the chopper and got on the radio.

"Warren, we thought you crashed or something." Walt's voice came through the speaker.

"No, we're all right, but Harris was knocked out by a tranquilizer dart from the object. I'll explain later. Right now we are stranded somewhere in the forest until Harris wakes up."

Fatal Abductions

"Try splashing some water on his face," Walt suggested.

"Hold on," he replied and looked around the chopper. He found a water bottle that Harris must have used and brought it to the man on the ground. He opened the bottle and sprinkled water on Harris. The man didn't stir.

"Great, now we just have to wait. What time is it?"

Dave looked at his watch and said, "Two-thirty. Think he'll be out long?"

"I don't know what they pumped him with. He could wake in minutes or hours. Check the medical kit under the pilot seat and see if there are any ammonia smelling salts."

Dave went to the chopper and pulled the kit out. He did find two vials of the salts and brought them to Warren. Warren took one, broke it open and held it under the pilot's nose. He started to stir and then moved his face quickly away from Warren's hand. He opened his eyes and they looked drugged.

"What the hell!" Harris yelled.

"Just don't move. They shot you with a tranquilizer dart. Rest for a bit. You've been out for a couple minutes."

"Minutes? I feel like I slept for a month. What the hell did they hit me with?" he said, still on the ground.

"Don't know until we get it examined. Rest until you can get up. Are you groggy or can you fly the chopper?" Warren asked.

"Give me a minute or two. My head is hurting."

"Alright, rest," Warren said and stood.

"Don't rush him. I don't want him passing out while we're in the air," Dave said.

"Got it. I better let Walt know what's happening." He went back to the chopper and got on the radio again. He relayed the information to Walt and said they'd be back as soon as possible.

Warren came back to Dave. "There aren't any bears in this area, are there?"

Dave laughed. "You have an arsenal of weapons in the chopper. Don't worry about bears."

"You know in all the excitement I forgot to even get a shot off at the thing." Warren was looking up for the object, but it was gone.

Dave said, "It may be good you didn't. We don't know if the five victims are in that thing."

"Okay, it was big and black. My spotlight didn't even show the surface. There were two propellers near the top that I could see before we took that dive. They weren't facing up, they were facing back. Which tells me they weren't for lifting the thing, more for pushing it forward."

"Like an air boat on water?" Dave asked.

"Yeah, this thing is more like a blimp, held up by helium and pushed around by the props."

Fatal Abductions

"Like the Goodyear blimp?" Dave asked.

"Yeah, just like that, only it seemed bigger."

The pilot sat up and groaned. "What happened? I remember being in a light, then a sharp pain, then nothing until I woke here."

"You got hit by the light. Dave jumped in to knock you away. There was someone else in the light with you. He, or it, must have shot you with the dart to knock you out."

"Damn, they couldn't have done that thing Spock does by grabbing my shoulder to knock me out. That dart hurt like a bitch."

"At least they didn't get you. The machine flew away after the other person in the light flew up," Warren said.

"Maybe he, or it, was pulled up by a cable?" Dave said.

"Could be. It's still a mystery, but we are gaining on it," Warren said and turned to the pilot. "You feel any better?" he said, helping the man up.

"Whoa, slow. I feel like a long night of drinking."

"Sit in your chair in the chopper and rest a bit longer." Warren helped him to the chair and he sat. Warren turned back to Dave. "I'm thinking this may be a job for the Air Force. Get a few jets to take the thing down."

"Not if our missing persons are aboard it. There's an eight year old boy still in there. I don't want some hotshot jet jockey taking the saucer out for the glory of it," Dave said. "So far it's just kidnapping a few people. If it starts shooting death rays, then call the Air Force."

"Okay. I'll hold off until we know what's going on."

The pilot yelled to them that he felt good enough to fly. They all got in and Harris started the chopper up and flew back to the house.

Warren called ahead and said they were coming back. "Tell Mike and Virgil to keep watch if the thing comes back."

Walt's voice came over the speaker, "Mike said the object took off back north really fast. Then it was out of sight. I think it's gone for the night."

Warren said, "I don't trust it, keep them watching for now. Just in case. They didn't get a third person tonight so they may try again."

The chopper followed the GPS of the van and arrived back at the house then landed.

Dave and Warren got out and helped Harris from his seat. Walt and Sarah came up and Warren said, "Take Harris into the house and put him on the couch." Alex went to help them.

"Now what, super-agent?" Dave said to Warren.

Fatal Abductions

"We have to regroup and plan better. We know a little of what to expect now, so we need to adapt. Most of tonight was a surprise. We need to be prepared for a second wave."

"If there is a second wave. I hope the thing doesn't move out of the area now that we've gotten so close to it," Dave said.

"Again, all we can do is wait. You may need to find a couple more men to man the towers. I don't think Mike and Virgil will be able to stay up two nights," Warren said as they walked to the house.

Walt and Sarah had Harris reclined on the couch, resting. The pilot still looked woozy. Sarah and Alex came to Dave and then Alex asked, "Any sign of my brother?"

"Alex, we were lucky to have even seen the thing. No sign of anyone, human or otherwise," Dave answered.

"So it is a flying saucer?" Sarah asked.

"I didn't say that. It had propellers so it can only fly in the atmosphere, not in space. No air. It was more of a blimp than a saucer."

"So this is the work of bad men taking people?" Alex said.

"It looks that way. We just need to figure how to stop the blimp and get on board. We had a run in with it tonight. Now we know what to expect," Dave told the boy.

"What are you going to do next?" Sarah asked.

Warren said, "I want to shoot it down, but Dave had to be logical and say we don't have the missing people back yet. They could be on the thing."

"Can't you figure out where something that big would land or hide?" Alex asked.

Walt spoke now. "I'll call the nearest base and see if we can get a recon plane to fly the area and see if they can spot it. It does have to land sometime."

"They probably have one of those secret bases inside a mountain that they fly into and park," Sarah said.

Dave laughed and said, "Again, you watch too many movies."

*

Chapter 10

Walt went to his electronic sanctum after asking Alex if he'd like to watch. The boy eagerly followed him to the van.

"Now what?" Dave asked Warren.

"We wait. Can you get some more people involved with spotting the thing?"

Fatal Abductions

"I can call on the volunteers who do searches for people lost in the woods. They might like watching for space ships," he said back.

"Sure, start a panic. Just say we have an enemy aircraft from a foreign country stealing our people."

"That'll work too. I'll have Mike call his contacts and get it started," Dave said and pulled out his cell phone.

Sarah went outside to the van to watch Walt call the Air Force. Dave explained to Mike what he wanted him to do then hung up. He told Warren about the call.

"Okay, all we can do now is wait again. If this thing shows up, we'll know what to expect," Warren said.

Walt came back into the house followed by Sarah and Alex. "I got some action on a recon plane for tomorrow morning early. They'll sweep the area with everything they got, radar, sonar, heat seeking…the whole shebang. If this thing is hiding out in the mountains, they'll find it."

"Good. Now we can get some rest. It's after four in the morning and I'm frankly wiped out," Warren said.

"You're always wiped out," Dave said with a laugh. "You'll need to find a place to sleep now that Harris has the couch. I guess you get the sleeping bag on the floor."

Warren quietly mumbled, "Crap."

Everyone was sleeping again. Van Gogh was wandering around the house when he jerked his head towards the back of the house looking out the huge windows. He started barking at a figure in the back yard by the windows of the house. The figure suddenly moved away upon hearing the dog barking. Van Gogh had his front paws up on the glass as he yipped at the intruder.

The figure went around to the helicopter and did something then went down by the water and climbed into a boat with two other figures. The boat took the men off from the breakwater wall. It quietly skimmed out and vanished down the shore.

Dave came out of the bedroom to Van Gogh. "What's the problem, dog?" He went to the windows and looked out, seeing nothing. "Are the squirrels playing this late? Come on, you can sleep in the bedroom. That'll keep you from bothering everyone." He took the dog's collar and pulled him away from the window. They went to the bedroom and Dave closed the door.

Early in the morning Harris was up and out to the helicopter, getting it ready to fly. Warren came out and asked, "Aren't you going to need to fuel it up?"

"That's what I'm preparing to do. There's a small airport south of here that has fuel. They store a couple choppers there already so they have the right fuel. I'll be back in a short while. I may take a quick fly over the area to see if I can spot anything."

"Good idea. See you soon," Warren said and moved back as Harris started the chopper up. Dave, Sarah and Alex came out and stood on the porch watching. Walt was standing by his van.

Fatal Abductions

Harris lifted up about twenty feet when the chopper suddenly lurched to the right. Harris was struggling to keep it up and then the thing shot towards the water, coming very close to the house by a few feet.

Dave grabbed Sarah and Alex and pulled them back away from the erratic flight of the chopper. It clipped a tree next to the house just before it banked towards the water and out past the breakwater. It nosedived into the water and stopped.

Everyone ran to the water's edge. Dave and Warren went to Dave's small boat moored at the dock. Dave started the motor and they ran it out to the chopper.

"He's lucky the water here is shallow. Another thirty feet further and it would have sunk below the surface," Dave yelled to Warren over the motor's noise.

They could see Harris trying to swim next to the chopper half sticking above the water. The cockpit was underwater and the tail was sticking straight up in the air.

Dave steered up to Harris as Warren reached out to the man. He climbed aboard the boat and Dave headed back to the shore.

"What the hell happened?" Warren asked the dripping man.

"Damned if I know. I got it up and then the controls froze. I was lucky it went into the water and not into the house."

Bob Moats

They got to the shore and Walt, with Sarah, helped Harris out of the boat. Dave tied it off as Warren and the others headed to the house. Dave stood looking at the chopper's tail sticking up like a tower. He followed the others into the house as Sarah poured Harris a cup of coffee.

"I don't know why it did that. I checked everything before starting the thing up," Harris said. "It was like I had no control over the tail rotors. I'll check it out again when we can get it out of the water."

"I'll call Mick's towing in town. He probably can tow it up and out of the water," Dave said.

"Short of bringing in a transport chopper to lift it out, that's probably the best idea for now," Warren said.

Dave went to make the call as Warren got a blanket from the couch and handed it to Harris standing in the vestibule. Sarah brought him a couple towels and told him to sit at the dining table. Harris toweled his face and head and sat looking from the dining area through the living room to the windows. He could see the tail sticking up from the water.

"I've never lost a chopper. I had hoped I could make retirement without dropping one," he said with a half-smile.

"You're lucky you weren't killed," Sarah said.

"I'm not believing this was coincidence. I have to examine it closely to see if it was sabotaged," Harris said.

Fatal Abductions

"Well, none of us would have done it," Warren said.

"I'm sure you guys wouldn't. I'm wondering if our invaders from space may have done it. I'll know better when we get it out."

Dave came back and said, "Mick is going to bring his five-ton wrecker over. He uses that for towing the big rig semi-trucks that break down, so it should be able handle the chopper."

Warren said, "I'll call HQ and explain to them about this and see if we can get another one out here. I'm sure they won't be happy." He pulled his cell phone out and went to the porch for privacy.

"Mick said he'd be right over, he's not busy today," Dave told Harris. "I have some dry clothes you can use. Come with me and I'll get you set up." The two men went to the bedroom.

"Wow, that was exciting," Alex said.

"Just be glad the thing didn't run into us and the house. That wouldn't be exciting," Sarah said.

About a half hour later, Mick showed up with a very huge tow truck. Dave showed him the situation.

"I've towed some strange things but never a helicopter. This should be interesting," Mick said with a big smile.

Mick backed his truck up to the breakwater wall and pulled out the heavy cable. Dave along with Harris brought the boat around and took the cable from Mick. He and Harris went out and attached the cable to a point that Harris said would stand the pulling by the tow truck.

Dave signaled Mick to start pulling slowly. Harris was watching to make sure the pull didn't damage the chopper further. Luckily it came out nicely. As the chopper got closer to the shore Harris was asking Dave to move closer so he could see if it would lift out of the water safely.

Mick raised the tow boom to lift the chopper up and then pulled it up until there was no more cable out of the boom. The chopper was mostly above the shore but Warren, Walt and Alex helped to guide it over the breakwater wall.

Mick drove forward and after Dave docked the boat, he said to put it in the front yard. The chopper was being dragged upright on its skids to the front yard where Mick lowered it. He came out of the cab and detached the cable.

"Mick, thanks for this. Send me the bill and I'll have the Feds pay it," Dave said.

"No charge, Dave. This was something to add to my resume." He laughed and went to leave.

Harris was examining the chopper, looking everywhere there were control cables or linkage. He took his time and finally he got to the tail rotors. He was checking out the control rods when he saw it.

"Warren, come here," he said.

"Find something?" Warren asked.

"Yep, and this was sabotage," Harris said. "Look at this rod that controls the rotors. It's been sawed through just enough until it would snap when I managed the controls. Just enough to get me in the air and then crash. If I hadn't gone into the water, who knows what would have happened if I hit the ground or the house?"

Warren looked at Dave and said, "Crap. Now we have a new mystery."

*

Chapter 11

"Destruction of government property by sabotage. I have to report this. It may help to get a few more agents out here to investigate," Warren said.

"Anything to keep you from working hard," Dave said with a laugh.

"I always work hard. But we need more eyes on this. I'll call and report the sabotage and get another chopper out here for tonight. If the aliens did this then they still have plans to hang around."

"Easy with the alien thing. I don't need that any more than I needed the zombies," Dave said. "I think you're right, they must have more to do here and they didn't like the chopper interfering. Something I don't understand. If they just wanted a few people, why didn't they grab them off the streets in a van or car?"

"I wondered that too. Maybe they're testing this airship and taking the people is a dry run for something worse," Warren said.

"I'd hate to think what could be worse," Walt said, standing next to Dave. "They evidently don't have death rays so they came here by foot to damage the chopper to keep us away. I guess they don't know we have an army of choppers at our disposal," Walt said and excused himself, going to his van.

"True, I may see if we can get a couple out here, just in case. And put guards on them this time," Warren said.

Harris came over and said, "Guys, this couldn't have been aliens from outer space. Whoever sawed through that rod had to know something about helicopters. They had to know which rod to cut for the most destruction and how far to cut it to keep it from breaking too soon. If I had been up in the air 500 feet and pushed the stick hard it would have snapped up there. I'd be in a metal sculpture."

"Well, lucky again that it broke before you got up high. Twice now you have survived possible death. One more and you get the trifecta award," Warren said.

Fatal Abductions

"I'm not even thinking about a third time. I'm covering my ass now." He laughed and went back to the chopper.

"He's right. This was no alien breaking your equipment. This was an old school attack on us. Just like cutting the brake lines on our cars. Maybe we should check them too," Dave said.

"Not a bad idea," Warren said.

Dave looked at Van Gogh. "The dog was going crazy around five-thirty. I should have figured something was up. Next time I'll let the dog loose to attack our intruders," Dave said.

Walt came back and said, "I called to reinforce your call to get another helicopter. They said it would be later today. Also, there are five agents driving out to help."

"Good, we should be ready for the aliens now," Warren said with a smile.

~~*~~

George was walking around the room examining the walls. He hoped to find an opening but saw none. It was strange that there were no doors or windows. He came to the cot where the young boy was sleeping and stood watching him breathe softly. He felt sorry that such a young child was taken from his family and friends. George was also missing his wife.

"So did you find a way out?" came a voice from behind him.

George turned to face the man on his cot. "You know damn well I didn't. You haven't found one either. Other than that slot where our food is shoved through, there's no other way out. I'm too big to slip through that slot."

"Then why do you keep looking?" came another voice from a toilet built into the wall. "You know this is a cell. We are prisoners and we had no trial. So give up looking. You're making me nervous." The man stood and pulled up his pants.

George stood staring at the man and said, "I survived the Korean War as a prisoner of war. I didn't stop looking for an escape. It was the one thing that kept me going. I found one, and six of us escaped to freedom. So I'm not giving up. If you aren't going to help, then shut up."

George went to his cot and sat, still looking around. He heard a tiny voice from his right and turned to see the boy looking at him. "Are we going home, Mr. George?"

"Yes, we will. I'll figure a way out. And I'm sure the law is looking for us. Don't you worry, we'll get home again," George said softly.

"Stop lying to the boy," came a voice from a man lying on a fifth cot.

Fatal Abductions

"I don't lie. I'm going to get us home. You wait and see," George said.

The slot at the bottom of the door opened and in slid trays of food. George went to the slot and grabbed at the hand that was pushing the trays in. He got hold of the hand, but his arm was pulled out through the slot and he felt a sharp pain, causing him to release the hand he grabbed. He fell back into the room holding his arm. The boy ran to him and yelled at the slot, "You're mean to do that."

George looked at his arm and saw the red welts from something they hit him with.

One of the men got up, went to George and looked at the wound. "They got you with a Taser. I've seen that before. They aren't playing around."

~~*~~

The extra agents arrived about twenty minutes after the second chopper landed. The pilot of the new chopper and Harris were looking at the damage to the first chopper.

"Yep, it was sabotage," the second pilot said.

"Well, I wouldn't have figured that out if you hadn't told me, Sam," Harris said with a grin.

"So what is this mysterious craft that is terrorizing the greater Seattle area?"

"It's nothing to sneeze at. I've seen it and almost got wiped out by it." Harris explained the whole situation to Sam.

"It's not aliens. I've heard of an organization that is making huge blimps and no one knows why."

"What organization is that?" Warren asked, standing behind the pilots.

Sam turned and said, "I heard through the Undernet that a whole bunch of rich men are planning on taking over the world. They will do it from the skies."

"Undernet, I haven't heard that term in a long time," Warren said.

"It's still out there. You just have to know where to find the right places to learn all this."

"I'm not into chatting with people. I stopped using the IRC years ago," Warren said.

"Yeah, well, there are people out there who know these things. It's easy to stay anonymous online in a chat room. You can tell everyone the worst things in the world and get away with it. I've heard about this organization of rich fat cats who want to take over the world."

"If you are talking about the Illuminati or the Bilderbergs or any one of a dozen groups who want to control the world, it's been done and not succeeded."

Fatal Abductions

"No, this is another group of people. All high up in finance and have the money," Sam said.

"They have a name?"

"Nope, but they are dangerous, so I hear. One person mentioned the Neo-Nazis and their quest to change the world."

"I don't want to hear about them. Give me another name, something less violent."

"Okay, there was mention of the Wall Street Ten. Bankers and investors who have money in the billions. It's been mentioned about them taking over the world," Sam said.

"The bureau has agents watching everywhere. Why haven't I heard about this?" Warren asked.

"Maybe they need to check out the old ways of the internet. There's a lot of stuff on the Internet Relay Chat."

"I'll mention it to the Director," Warren said with a smile, excused himself and went back to the extra agents who were unpacking the SUVs.

"Did you bring enough baggage?" Warren asked the men.

One agent said, "We weren't told how long we would be out here."

"Okay, put it all back in the car. You're going to a motel. Then back here to get ready for our mission."

The men put everything personal back in the car as Dave came over to Warren.

"I called and got them rooms in the same motel from last time you invaded the area. I have Mike still up in the tower, so you and I will have to lead them to the motel."

"No problem," Warren said as Dave's cell phone rang.

He looked at the ID. It was Mike. He answered and listened. "Good, Mike. Come to the house and take these new agents to the Lookout Motel, then you and Virgil go home and get some sleep." He hung up.

"The relief spotters are up in the towers now. So my men can go rest now. What's the word from the Air Force about the recon plane?"

"They did a sweep of the entire area and up through the mountains to the coast. They got nothing. No blimp on the ground or floating around. Maybe Sarah was right about the thing pulling into a mountain hole and parking," Warren said.

"I'll tell her you agree. So we wait now for night and hope they do another raid." Warren was watching the men doing something to the new helicopter. He and Dave went over to see.

"Are those missiles?" Warren asked as the pilots were pulling a tarp off the weapons.

Harris said, "Yep. If we need it, we have it. Better than not have it."

Chapter 12

"Well, I'm all for it after seeing that thing, but there will be no launching the missiles unless I say so. Understood?"

Both pilots agreed. "You say the word and we'll take this thing down," Harris said. "After seeing it, I know there is a danger. You give the word, and we'll take care of it."

"Good. I'm glad someone took the initiative to send this along. Now get this bird ready for flight. Hopefully we fly tonight." Warren smiled and took Dave with him as he went to the house. "I need a drink," he said.

"A little early in the day, don't you think?" Dave asked.

"It's to help me sleep until tonight." They went in the house and found Sarah with Alex in the kitchen.

"Hey, hon, did you get the cavalry ready to fight?" Sarah asked.

"We're ready to fight tonight. What are you two up to?" Dave asked his wife as he gave her a big kiss on the cheek.

"We're making sandwiches for everyone," she replied.

"Sandwiches?" Dave asked.

"Yes, we haven't had a lunch yet so we are feeding our friends."

Dave realized they hadn't eaten. "Must be the anticipation. We forgot to eat. Good of you to feed us."

"Well, you need to have food to keep going," Sarah said.

"I need a drink," Warren said.

Dave laughed and pulled him to the living room. "Sit. I'll get you whatever you want."

"A beer would work for me right now."

"I'll get one for each of us," Dave said and went to the fridge to get the drinks. He headed back to the living room passing Sarah who gave him the eye.

"We're relaxing," Dave told her. She went back to the sandwiches and just snorted. Dave laughed.

Dave handed Warren his beer and sat. "So are you having fun yet?"

"I'm ready to retire from this business," he said.

Dave looked at his friend and said, "Are you being serious or just being yourself?"

"No, I'm serious. I'm getting to the point where I'm not crazy about chasing serial killers, terrorists, zombies and now aliens. The outer space kind or the human kind. It's no fun anymore." He took a swig of the beer and put his head back on the chair.

"That doesn't sound like you," Dave said.

Warren raised his head and said, "You have a home, a wife, a dog and a happy life. Other than when you have serial killers, terrorists, zombies or aliens." He started laughing, then stopped. "I'm wishing I had a wife like Sarah. She's a great woman, and if I could shoot you and take her away, I would. But she'd never agree to that."

"You've had women in your life. Pick one and settle."

Warren took another big swig and said, "That's the problem, I can't settle. I think I need to get away from the FBI so maybe I can feel safe enough to settle. But every time I go out on a case I don't know if I'll come back alive. What kind of life would that be for a wife?"

"Warren, my job is just as bad. I could stop a speeder and get shot just as easily. Law enforcement, no matter which branch, is prime for death. You'd have to get out of the FBI completely to be safe. You could join a private security firm and guard buildings, but I don't think you could do that."

"I know. Maybe you'd need another deputy?"

"My budget wouldn't allow it. If I could, you'd be on my team," Dave said.

Walt came into the living room. "Mike is here, Dave."

"Thanks, Walt." Dave said then stood and turned to Warren. "Don't quit until we solve this mystery. I need you. Now I'll go get Mike set up with delivering your men to the motel. Just relax and think a while."

Dave left the room and went out to Mike. He explained what needed to be done and got the agents ready to leave. They departed and Dave stood in the driveway watching the two men working on the helicopter.

Dave suddenly jumped when an arm came around him with a sandwich in its hand. "Damn, you need to have a bell around your neck," he said as Sarah came around him. He took the sandwich and ate a big bite.

"So what's up with Warren?" she asked.

"He's feeling lonely. We need to find him a woman. He wants to retire from the bureau and settle down."

"Warren? Settle down? I don't see that happening anytime soon. But I can see if I can find a girlfriend for him."

"You don't know any woman that Warren would like. He's picky."

"Beggars can't be choosy. I'll get him settled." She kissed Dave and went back to the house.

"Poor Warren," Dave said to himself.

A half hour later the agents returned to the house and Warren explained what they would be doing. He assigned two men to watch the helicopter in case of another attack.

Fatal Abductions

The other three men were told to be ready to go up in the chopper to help with tracking the aircraft. He told them to get some rest because it could be a long night. They went to the step van that they came in and pulled out a canopy. Then they pulled out cots and spread them out under the canopy.

Dave made a call to the men in the towers to see how they were holding up. He told them that Mike and Virgil would be back out to help watch.

Warren had already relaxed in the recliner in the living room when Dave came in. Alex was resting on the couch, so Dave went to sit next to him.

"Do you think we'll find my brother?" Alex asked.

"I'm hoping for the best, but it's good to realize that we may not find him. So prepare yourself for that too. But don't lose hope."

"I wish we had never been out that night. I blame myself," Alex said looking upset.

"Can't take blame for what you had no control over. You had to go on with your lives, and you couldn't hide in your house forever. Going out of your home every day is a risk. So don't take it so hard."

"Thanks. It's hard to live in our house with mom. She makes life miserable."

"Well, as I said before, I'll see what I can do about that," Dave said and gave Alex a smile.

Bob Moats

Everyone was resting. Sarah and Dave in the bedroom, Alex in the guest room and Warren on the couch. The rest of the men were out under the canopy on cots. It was quiet.

One agent wasn't sleeping; he was guarding the choppers. He watched it get dark and then he sat on a folding chair they'd brought. He was trying to stay awake, then he heard a low buzzing noise. He stood and went out to the center of the yard looking around, trying to get a fix on the sound.

Harris lifted his head from the cot just in time to see the agent bathed in the beam of light. Harris yelled to the others and jumped up running towards the light. But the light vanished and so did the agent.

"Damn!" he yelled again as the other agents and Sam came running up. "Go get Warren now!" he yelled to the agents and turned to Sam. "Get the chopper warmed up quickly."

Sam ran to the chopper and started the procedure for starting it up. Shortly Warren came barreling out of the house followed by Dave and the agents.

"What the hell happened? They told me a light took Frank. How did it get here without being seen?" Warren was trying not to get angry.

"I looked up from the cot when I heard a noise and saw Frank standing in the yard. Then the light hit him and he was gone. I couldn't get to him in time. Sam is getting the chopper ready."

Fatal Abductions

Warren, Dave and Harris ran to the chopper and the rest of the men piled in. They were in the air in minutes and flew around getting their bearings.

Dave called the towers on his cell phone and asked how they missed the craft. He was told they couldn't see anything. It was foggy over the mountains and visibility was poor. He relayed the message to Warren.

"Great, we have another bad break. Sam, see what you can find on the radar. Any big object up here with us."

"I've already got it working, but nothing on the scope. Not one single object in the sky," Sam said.

"More bad news. Are we ever going to catch a break on this?" Warren said. "Sam, keep circling around. Hopefully we'll run into the thing."

Harris said, "I hope we don't run into it, just find it."

"That's what I meant," Warren said with a smile. "I'm not going down in flames yet."

They flew around the area until the fog moved in closer. "I'm running on instruments, visibility is getting bad. I may need to land soon," Sam said.

"Okay, follow the GPS of Walt's van and get us safely home." Warren wasn't happy that they lost a man and the airship in one night.

"This can't keep up. We have to find where it lands. We'll organize a search in the morning and really scour the mountains. It has to be there somewhere. It's the only place they could hide," Warren said. "Do you have grid maps of the area?" he asked Dave.

"I have some geological maps that should help."

"Good, I'll see if we can get anything from our spy in the sky satellites. They can penetrate most ground cover if the thing is inside a mountain," Warren said. "Plus, that thing has to be manned by humans. The satellites can get a heat signature off them."

Dave smiled and said, "If they're human."

*

Chapter 13

The four men and the young boy were sitting on their cots in the windowless room. None of them were talking, just resting. There wasn't much else to do.

"I think even prisoners get some kind of entertainment, like magazines. These are some lousy jailers," the biggest of the men said.

"Jack, stop complaining. We aren't going anywhere, so just shut up," another man said.

"Steve, you can sit there and dream about whatever. I can't take not having anything to do. I need something to take my mind off being in here for God knows how many days," Jack said.

The third man looked at his watch. "We've been here for five days. The old man and the kid have been here almost three days."

"Well, thank you for the report. I'm glad someone is paying attention," Jack said sarcastically.

"This place could be anywhere. In Seattle or out in the bay area. I think we are somewhere we won't be found," Steve said. "Why us? Do we have something they want? I don't have any money, so that can't be it. I have no rich parents or any parents at all. They have a lousy hostage in me."

"Maybe they want you for your brain, asshole," Jack said. "This cage is very strange. No way in or out. The old man and kid just popped up while we were asleep, so I didn't even see how they got in." He turned to George. "Do you remember how you got in here?"

"All I remember is the light around me and then a sharp pain. That was all until I woke in here," George said.

"Same here," the third man said. "I'm Ed, by the way. I don't know why I'm here either. I'm a fireman and I was out in my backyard with my dog when that light hit me too. What do you do, George?"

"I have a horse ranch. My daughter does most of the work. She takes care of the horses for me. I'm retired as far as I'm concerned," George answered.

"Well, a horse rancher and a fireman. So what are you Jack?" Steve asked.

Jack didn't answer. The others waited for him, then he said, "If you must know I'm a car thief. I steal cars to take to a chop shop and make my money. I'm a very good car thief. Until that stinking light caught me. I thought it was the cops, but they don't have cells like this. What are you, Mr. Nosey?"

"I'm a cop. But don't worry, I won't arrest you. Seems we are all under arrest here. Except the kid, he's just visiting," he said, looking at Jeffrey. "Aren't you, kid?"

Jeffrey looked like he wanted to cry. "Leave the boy alone. It's bad enough he's in here with us. He should be home with his family," George said.

There was a rumbling noise then one wall started to move. It slid slowly open horizontally to about eight feet wide then stopped. It was pitch black outside the room.

Jack was on his feet and headed to the opening when a man in military fatigues stepped from the side with an automatic rifle. Jack stopped. Then another man came from the other side of the opening. He also had a weapon.

"What's going on here and why are we being held? This is illegal, you know!" Jack yelled at the men.

"You are prisoners of the New World Order," came a voice from behind one of the men. A man in a more formal uniform stepped up followed by two other men dragging a lifeless man. They dropped him in the room and went back out. Steve stood, went to the unconscious man and checked him.

The formal man said, "He's alive. Don't worry, we need all of you alive. I hope your accommodations are adequate."

"Screw you!" Jack yelled. "Why are we here and who the hell is the New World Order?"

The formal man smiled and waved his hand. The wall started to move again to close.

"Have a nice visit, gentlemen," the man said.

George stepped up and yelled, "At least let the boy go!"

"Oh no, we need him too," the man said as the wall shut.

"What the hell?" Steve said. "New World Order? That's a bunch of bull conspiracy theory. There's not enough men in the world together who can take over the world. He's lying."

"Well, we don't have much else to go on do we, officer?" Jack mocked. Steve moved towards the big man, but George stepped in his way.

"Hey, instead of fighting, we know how the room works now. Why don't we figure how to get out?"

Steve glared at Jack but moved back away from George. "I'm all for getting out. But you saw those weapons. There's probably guards on the outside willing to shoot us."

"The head man said they needed the boy too. So they need us alive. Now who is this guy on the floor?" George bent down and shook the man slightly. The man stirred. He opened his eyes and when he focused he jumped up quickly.

"Where the hell am I?" he said.

"Same thing I've been asking," Jack said. "And just who are you?"

"Special Agent Frank Michaels, FBI," he said.

"Well, we have a cop and now a Fed. I'm feeling outnumbered," Jack said.

Steve went to the agent and said, "Don't mind him, he's a lowly car thief."

Jack lunged for Steve but the agent grabbed his arm and twisted it behind his back. "Now just settle down or I'll pop your arm out of its socket."

"Okay, okay! Stop twisting!" Jack howled.

Michaels pushed Jack to the side and held his hand out to Steve. "A cop, eh? Now I don't feel so bad about being captured so easily."

"Do you know where we are?" George asked.

"Are you George?" he asked.

Fatal Abductions

"I am and how did you know?"

"This must be Jeffrey," he said, smiling at the boy.

"Again, sir, how do you know?" George asked.

"We've been looking for you." He turned to the others and said, "All of you since you disappeared around the Seattle area. Unfortunately, now they are going to be looking for me."

"They got you in a beam of light too?" Ed asked.

"I was guarding a helicopter when the airship got me."

"Airship? What airship?" George asked.

"I haven't seen it. I just arrived in the area today. But I was told there's a very big blimp-like object that floats around and is picking off people from the ground. I guess we are them."

"Do the Feds know where we are?" Steve asked.

"They're still trying to track the airship down. I'm sure it will be a matter of time before they find it. How did I get in here?" Michaels asked.

"The wall opened and they dragged you in here. Until now we didn't know how to get in or out," Steve said.

"Do you know if we're in the airship or on the ground? Has this room seemed to move?"

"No, we've been stationary as far as I can tell," Steve said.

"Good, that means we are in some base somewhere. I hope my friends can find us."

~~~*~~~

In the dining room, Warren was having fits. "We now have one of our agents taken! I'm not happy about this!"

"Warren, it happened. There no use in having a coronary," Dave said.

"I'd welcome a coronary right now. When the field director hears about this, my ass is grass, and he's the lawnmower."

Walt said, "I think I have some good news."

Warren stood staring at him, "Well, are you going to tell us now or after we find the blimp?"

"Oh, yeah. When all of the agents arrived I equipped them with trackers in their belts. Now if he isn't searched real close, they may not find it. We can track him that way," Walt explained.

"Finally, some good news. Can you get his location?"

"Well, there is some bad news," Walt said.

Fatal Abductions

"Crap, I knew it was too good."

"The range on the tracker is about two miles, so we need to fly around to find the signal."

"Okay, that's still in the good news category. You go up with Harris and Sam with your spooky equipment and see if you can find the signal. If you do, get the coordinates and come back. Then I'll bring in the marines to attack them. Go!" he yelled.

The three men went out as Dave looked at his watch. "It's almost one in the morning and it's foggy. It would be better to wait until daylight for them to go."

Warren stood looking helpless. "Yeah, no sense in them crashing into a mountain. Everhart, go tell them to wait," he said to the nearest agent. The man left the room.

"At least you have a man on the inside now," Dave said.

"Yeah and Michaels is a good agent. He'll find a way to get them out from the inside," Warren said and sat at the dining table. "I hope."

"Did Walt give you one of those trackers?" Sarah asked Warren.

"No, he hasn't," Warren answered.

"Hmm...I guess he doesn't want to find you," she said with a smile.

"You know, you can be annoying when you want," Warren said.

"I do my best."

Walt came back in and said, "We'll go as soon as the sun comes over the horizon. It is still foggy out there."

Warren put his head in his hands and said, "I hope that means they won't be flying anymore tonight either." He looked at Walt and said, "I need to have a talk with you about these trackers."

*

Chapter 14

FBI agent Frank Michaels was listening at the wall where he was told it opened. He was saying that he could hear nothing.

Jack came over and started banging on the wall hard.

"Hey, don't do that!" Michaels said.

"You want to know if there's someone out there, make some noise and they'll tell us to shut up," Jack said.

Michaels smiled at the thought and started to bang on the wall also. After about two minutes of pounding, there still was no response.

Fatal Abductions

Steve was standing behind the men. "Maybe we aren't being guarded. Maybe they figure we can't get out so they don't have to watch us."

Michaels looked around the room and then bent down to study a cot. It had a metal frame holding the cloth bedding. He picked it up and started bending the whole thing.

"What the hell are you doing?" Jack asked.

"I need something like a crowbar to jimmy the wall. You said it slid aside, then it must be on tracks. Maybe if we apply enough pressure, we may be able to move it."

Jack came over and started to help break apart the cot. Finally after much twisting and bending they broke off a piece of metal bar about six feet long and sturdy. Michaels went to the corner of the room and was working the bar into the crack where the walls met.

After ten minutes of jamming the bar into the wall, he succeeded in creating a hole in the corner. He jammed the bar through the hole and told Jack to help him pull the bar to make the moveable wall open. They pulled and pulled then finally they heard a movement in the wall.

It separated from the opposite wall by a crack, just enough to get their hands into and pull it further. The other men came over and helped pull the wall until they managed to get it open by less than a foot. Then it stuck. There was no one stopping them, so they figured they were safe.

"Well, it's not enough for us to get through. There must be a switch out there that controls the door," Michaels said then looked at Jeffery. He turned to George and said, "Your little friend can squeeze through. Maybe he could find a control to open it all the way."

George looked at the boy and went to him. He knelt down and said, "Jeff, would you like to help us get out of here?"

The boy nodded.

"Okay, I'm going to ask you to go on a dangerous mission that will save us. Can you do that?"

The boy nodded again. George took the boy by the hand and led him to the corner.

Michaels bent down and said, "We need to find a button or lever that would open this wall. Do you think you can find one?"

"I can try," the boy said.

"Okay, squeeze through the opening and look around for a control panel or a switch."

Jeffrey went through the opening with a little help from Michaels. He was on the other side now and disappeared.

"Jeff, are you all right?" Michaels called to the boy. He heard a faint reply saying he was all right.

Fatal Abductions

The men were waiting patiently for a few minutes. They could hear the boy pushing and banging on things. "I hope he doesn't make enough noise to alert anyone," Steve said.

Suddenly the wall started to rumble and then it moved. The men quietly cheered and slipped out as the wall receded.

George went to Jeffery standing on a chair by a box with a handle marked 'Door' and took him down. "Good work, you have saved us."

"So far, but we're not out yet," Jack said.

~~*~~

Warren was pacing around the kitchen waiting for daylight. Dave came out of the bedroom, found him standing in the middle of the room and said, "Have you been up all morning? You'll fall asleep while we chase bad guys."

"I'll manage. I emptied Walt's supply of Red Bull. I'm a bit wired right now," Warren said with a big grin.

"Well, be careful who you shoot. Remember I'm one of the good guys," Dave said and got a cup of coffee from the automatic coffee maker.

"Is Sarah up yet?" Warren asked.

"She's been awake too. I think she's worried that the aliens will take over the world. I tried to get her to relax, but you know her."

The front door opened and in came Walt, looking a mess. He handed Warren a portable radio. "Have you brought a change of clothes?" Warren asked his partner.

"No. There was no more room in the van for baggage other than yours. Were you planning on staying a month?"

"I like to be prepared," Warren said, grinning.

"Harris and Sam are getting the chopper ready to fly. They had two men guarding the chopper this morning while they rested. It was too foggy, even for the blimp, so they figured we wouldn't be attacked."

"Good. Get up in the air and see if you can get a fix on the tracker signal. I'll wait back here for you to relay the coordinates. I've called a colonel friend from Bangor Base and alerted him that we may need help. He's got a couple transport choppers ready to fly with his troops," Warren said.

"Good, I'll go see if the guys are ready to fly." Walt went out.

Dave said, "It's starting. Shall we go watch them go up?"

The two men went out to the yard as the chopper was revving up. Sarah and Alex came out of the house to join them.

Fatal Abductions

"Think they'll find them?" Alex asked.

"If Michaels' tracker is still working they should," Warren replied. "We'll see."

Walt called from the chopper to test the radio that Warren had and it was working. He said he'd call as soon as they had something.

The helicopter's blades sped up and the thing lifted off. Everyone on the ground covered their eyes as the dust kicked up from the prop wash. The chopper was now heading north and then disappeared behind the trees on the property.

"All we can do is wait again," Warren said. "Shall we go get something to eat?"

"I'm not cooking, you can make your own eggs," Sarah said with a smile.

"I'm a guest, you should take care of me." Warren laughed.

"So you think. You are becoming a regular around here, so you can do your own cooking." She turned and went back to the house followed by Alex.

"You need to control your woman," Warren said to Dave.

Dave laughed and said, "Are you kidding? She controls me."

They went in the house after Warren tested the radio again. It worked fine, Walt replied.

~~*~~

Walt was consulting a map of the area, marking off the parts they had flown over. Harris was flying fairly low so they could pick up any signal from the tracker. Walt was checking his receiver for a signal but heard nothing.

"I hope they haven't found the tracker on Michaels. But we'll fly around and see what we can find," Walt told the pilots.

"I think we should go through the valleys between the mountains. It would have better cover for a blimp. If we start getting a signal I'll fly higher so we can get a visual sighting," Harris said.

Walt agreed and studied the map as they flew into the first valley.

"Hopefully they don't see us. They may have radar wherever they are," Sam said. "If they have the technology to put that thing in the air, they must have some security."

"I feel a little better with those missiles below us. I don't want to hurt the captives but that thing needs to be taken down," Harris said.

Fatal Abductions

"Just hold off until you hear from Warren," Walt said.

"In his absence you are senior agent here. You can make a decision too. Especially since Warren isn't here," Sam said.

Walt smiled and said, "We'll see."

Harris banked around a tall cliff in the mountain face and into another valley. Walt marked off the area as checked. He was watching the receiver for even a faint sound from the tracker.

They flew for about an hour and covered a couple hundred miles of mountain range. Still no sounds from the receiver.

"Could they be covered by something that's disrupting transmissions?" Harris asked.

"It's possible. Maybe we can't see them because they are covered by something that shields them from spying eyes," Walt said. "The recon plane found nothing from above."

"Just how big is this thing?" Sam asked.

"Can't tell. It's so dark that we couldn't see the entire thing. But we estimate it's probably around the length of a football field. Small for an airship," Harris said. "The Hindenburg was 804 feet long, almost three football fields."

"You think it's a blimp?" Sam asked.

"Best guess it is. There are propellers on the top to push it forward and possibly back. I've only seen it once, and that's as much as I got out of it."

"They'd have to refill the helium, and helium is getting scarce as I understand it. They'd be crazy to fill it with hydrogen. Look at what that did to the Hindenburg," Sam said.

"Which is why I don't understand the whole idea of using a blimp. Expensive to maintain and hard to maneuver," Walt added.

Suddenly the receiver was making a noise. Walt yelled, "It's the tracker signal. We got it!"

*

Chapter 15

Harris took the chopper up higher to see if they could spot the blimp. Walt was still trying to pinpoint the signal to get a fix on the location. They couldn't see anything on the ground resembling a black blimp.

Walt said, "The signal seems to be moving. Do you see anything on the ground below us?"

"There's a road down there. It's long and goes nowhere. I think I see a vehicle moving along it. Shall I go down for a closer look?" Harris asked.

Fatal Abductions

"Closer, but not too close," Walt replied.

Harris took the chopper down trying to keep it directly above the car so whoever was in it wouldn't spot them.

"It looks like an Army jeep, the boxy kind they used in World War II," Sam said, looking through the Plexiglas opening in the front of the chopper.

"They don't have much room in those vehicles. Could they get all six of the hostages in it?" Walt asked.

"It'd be tight, but not likely."

"Shall we take a run at them and see what's up?" Walt said.

Harris smiled at Walt and took the chopper into a dive in front of the jeep. He was now running just above the road and turned towards the vehicle as the jeep stopped. Walt hit the door and went out as Harris landed.

Both pilots had their weapons out as Walt moved out front of the chopper. There was no movement in the jeep. Walt could only see one person in the driver's seat.

The three men spread out as Walt yelled, "FBI! Get out of the jeep with your hands showing. Now!"

The driver didn't move, so Walt fired a warning shot by the jeep. The man opened the door and came out with his hands in front of him. He was unarmed. Walt moved up to him as did Harris and Sam. "Handcuff him while I get the tracker receiver."

Bob Moats

Walt went back to the chopper, took out the device and brought it to the jeep. He did a sweep of the vehicle and then ran it over the man. The signal went crazy as Walt scanned the man's pocket.

Harris reached in the pocket and came out with the tracker. "Damn! They found it." Walt brought his gun up to the man's face as he stood silent. "Where are they? The agent you took this device from and the others."

The man just smiled and said nothing. Walt went to the jeep to search it as Harris frisked the man. Walt found nothing of value that would tell them anything. He did find a box of groceries in the back. He figured the man was making a run for food. Harris took everything he found on the man and put the items in a plastic bag he had.

Walt turned back to Sam. "Sam, run the jeep off the road as far back as you can get it and then we'll take this asswipe back."

Sam drove the jeep off the side and into a grove of trees. It was hidden from the road. He came back as Harris and Walt were putting the man in the chopper. Walt got on his radio and called Warren, explaining what happened.

"Okay, take him to the sheriff's office. There's plenty of space to land. We'll meet you there," Warren's voice came over the radio. Then he clicked off.

Walt looked at Harris and said, "Record the coordinates so we can get back here."

The helicopter rose up and away from the site, heading back to the sheriff's office. Walt figured that

Fatal Abductions

Warren would drive the van there so he told Harris to track the GPS. Harris said the signal was moving so they followed it.

~~*~~

Warren parked the van in front of the sheriff's office as Dave pulled his Bronco in beside the van. They got out and went up the steps to the building.

"Great, the door is unlocked. We've probably been sacked." He went in and heard a noise. He had his gun out, as did Warren, and went down the hall to the counter. Mike was sitting at his desk.

"When did you get here?" Dave asked Mike.

"About an hour ago. I couldn't sleep so I came here. I talked to Willis up in the tower and he told me about the fog and losing an agent. Sorry, Warren."

"Thanks, Mike. But we do have a prisoner now. Walt's bringing him in by chopper," Warren said.

"Is he an alien?" Mike asked with a grin.

"Walt didn't say, but I'm sure he's human. He was driving an old army jeep."

"An alien with a driver's license, that's not good." Mike gave the men a big grin and stood. "Want me to call Virgil in?"

"May as well, we may need him to help," Dave said.

They were waiting when they heard the chopper approach. They all went out to the parking lot as the chopper landed at the edge of the lot by a field.

Walt got out and pulled the prisoner out, helped by Sam. Harris was shutting down the chopper. Warren, followed by Dave and Mike, came up.

Mike said, "He looks human."

Walt gave the prisoner a push towards Warren who grabbed his lapels and shook the man. "You know you have been involved in kidnapping six people including a child. That's a capital offense. You could get life in prison. How's that sound?"

The man still said nothing. "Okay, stone face, I'm offering you a deal. Tell us where the hostages are and I'll see you get off light on charges."

Still nothing.

"Come on, cat got your tongue?" Warren asked.

The man smiled and then opened his mouth. He had no tongue.

Warren was shocked and pushed the man back. "What the hell? Who did that to you?"

Fatal Abductions

Of course no answer, so Warren said to Mike, "Take him in and put him in your cell for now."

Warren turned to Dave. "That's one way to keep your men from talking. This must be a crazy bunch of nutjobs."

Walt came closer and said, "He was driving down a long road that Sam said was going nowhere. He had to be going somewhere."

"Maybe his base of operations? Did you find anything in the jeep?"

"No, just a box of groceries, but not enough to feed many people."

"Maybe he's a cook, just picking up supplies," Mike said.

"From where? He was miles out from any city," Dave said.

"Good question. Shall we question him? Bring a pad of paper. He can write I'm sure," Warren said.

They went into the building and took the man from the cell and into the conference room. The office wasn't big enough to have an interrogation room. Besides they didn't have enough crime to interrogate anyone.

As they organized the seating situation Virgil walked in. "Hey, what's going on?" he asked.

Mike turned to him and said with a smile, "We have an alien."

116

Bob Moats

Virgil's eyes went wide as Dave told him to go man the phones. Virgil left the room after doing a quick look at the prisoner. He shook his head and mumbled, "That doesn't look like an alien to me."

That broke the tension in the room. Everyone laughed except the prisoner.

Warren sat next to the guy. "Sergio, I checked your Nevada driver's license and that's your name. Handicapped it also says. I presume it's because you have no tongue. I also found a grocery list. You must have really needed the supplies because the nearest store was about 80 miles away. Were you getting those supplies for the men in the blimp?"

Sergio's eyes widened slightly, telling Warren he struck a nerve. "So you do know all about the blimp. What can you tell me about the people who run it?"

Warren pushed the pad and pencil to the man and waited. The man didn't move for a long time.

"Okay, we can just put you in a cell and leave you there until you think of something to tell us." Warren signaled to Mike to take him away. Mike took the man's arm and the man reached over and grabbed Mike's gun from its holster. Everyone jumped and drew their weapons as the man put the gun to his head and pulled the trigger. Before anyone could do anything the man was dead.

"Damn it!" Warren yelled. "Even handcuffed he did this."

Fatal Abductions

Dave told Mike to get Doc Mitchell, the coroner, to come take the body. Dave stood looking at the blood on the walls behind the victim.

"We are back to square one again. This sucks!" Warren was still upset. "Walt, what can we do now?"

Walt was looking pale and stuttered as he said, "Well, we can go back to where we found him and the jeep and do a search from there. He had to be heading back to their base of operations."

"Okay, that works for me. Did you get the coordinates so we can get back to where you found him?" Warren asked.

"I had Harris record them in case. We can get back where we left the jeep. I didn't expect this," Walt answered.

"Nobody expected this," Dave said.

Mike came back in the room. "The doc is coming over."

"Thanks, Mike. We need to get this mess cleaned up. Call Olympia and see if their crime scene clean-up people can get here quickly," Dave said.

Mike went back out as Virgil stood by the door looking at the mess. He came in and looked down at the body. Then he said, "I guess aliens have red blood, too."

*

Chapter 16

"Virgil, go back to your desk," Dave told his deputy.

Virgil grinned and left the room. Dave went out and turned to Warren as he came out. "We need to find out where Sergio was heading before Walt and the others stopped him. I'll need to see the map to be able to say where that road goes to."

Warren turned to Walt. "Go get your maps and show us where this jeep is."

Walt went out to get the map as they waited. Walt came back in followed by Doc Mitchell and two of his orderlies from the town clinic.

"Hey, Doc, we have a situation," Dave said to the man.

"Mike told me about it on the phone. Too bad you lost a prisoner. Mike said he may be an alien. Is that true?"

"Doc, don't go spreading that," Dave said as he looked over at Mike sitting at his desk, smiling. "You remember the zombie invasion. Let's not have an alien invasion now."

"Got ya, Dave. I'll have my men take him out quickly. Do you want an autopsy?"

"If it will do any good, why not? Let me know if you find anything," Dave said.

"Will do, Dave. I'll call later," he said and went to help his men bag the body.

Mike said, "I got the clean-up people coming out, but it won't be until tomorrow."

"Lock up the conference room until it gets cleaned," Dave told him.

Walt had the map spread out on the counter and Warren was studying it. Dave came up and Walt pointed to the area where they left the jeep. The three men were looking over the map and Dave was studying the area where the jeep was.

"Mike, can you come here?" Dave asked his deputy. Mike came to the counter and Dave said, "I think I know this road. It's one that goes out to an old mine. Do you know it?"

Mike read the label on the map as to the road and said, "Yeah, it's the road where teens used to drive out to party. I haven't been there in years. It's out of our jurisdiction. It's now part of the main Jefferson County Sheriff's jurisdiction."

"We are part of the Jefferson County Sheriff's Department, Mike. So I think it would be our jurisdiction. Besides this is now part of a federal investigation. So Warren can investigate it."

Warren smiled and said, "Shall we go out there and party?"

"You're no longer a teenager, Warren," Dave said.

"Doesn't stop me from thinking like one," he said with a grin.

"Yeah, you are still just a kid," Dave said. "Mike, watch the office. Virgil, come with us."

All the men went out to the chopper. Harris and Sam were standing by, waiting to go up.

"Harris, take us back to where you left the jeep," Warren said to the pilot. They all climbed in the chopper and Harris fired it up. Sam navigated them back to the coordinates of the road and they arrived about ten minutes later. They landed on the road where they had been earlier.

They got out and Harris said, "I parked the jeep behind those trees."

"Go bring it back," Warren said to the man. He walked off and a few minutes later he came back on foot.

"Where's the jeep?" Warren asked.

"Hell if I know. It's gone. I can see the tracks, but they go back out. Someone came and took it," Harris said.

"The aliens found it and took it back," Warren said with a grin. "Which way do the tracks go?" he asked.

Fatal Abductions

Harris pointed up the road into the valley. "That's the best I can determine. The tracks head that way."

Dave said, "Well, the other way goes towards the next town. The way the jeep goes is towards the mining town."

"What kind of mining?" Warren asked.

"About seventy years ago, someone thought there was gold out here. I don't know all the details, but they went bust. Not enough gold found to make it worth staying. This was a trail for wagons to reach the small town. It's a ghost town now. Over the years all the cars that drove out here to see the town caused the road to widen and become more of a flattened surface. Shall we go chase some ghosts?" Dave said.

"Or aliens," Virgil said with a big smile. Dave almost hit him.

~~*~~

Agent Michaels was going to lead the men into the dark corridors and hopefully out of the building he determined they were in. When they left their cell, he could vaguely see the rest of the room. In the glow of the cell lights he saw they were in the middle of a much larger room, more of a large school gym sized building. There were two doors that he could see in the semi-darkness. Everyone searched the area around the cell and then Steve found a tool box. He pulled four screwdrivers out and handed them to the men.

"You can use these as weapons if needed," he said.

Michaels found two flashlights. He gave one to Steve, the cop, and kept the other. "Okay, we need to get out of here. Let's try a door and see where it goes."

They went to the first, closest door and Michaels slowly opened it, looking out. He was amazed to see they were in a much larger area mostly made from rock. They were in what Michaels determined to be a large cavern of rock. They carefully came out and went along the wall of the cave toward a flat wall that looked like it was man-made. There were doors in the wall, but where they went to, Michaels had no idea. It was a starting point.

They carefully walked to the door, being hidden by stacks of boxes along the rock walls. Michaels stopped to look into one of the boxes and was shocked to see it contained automatic weapons. He checked another box and it had missiles for hand held launchers. He turned to Steve and said, "This is not good. We have to get out and warn people."

They got to the door and Michaels looked out. It was a smaller room that was more like an office building. They went through and were stopped by about ten men appearing with automatic weapons. They came from hidden spaces, which shocked the men. The formal man still in his uniform came from behind a door and said, "Very good that you got this far. Our escape test has been fruitful. Take them to the new cell," he told his men.

Fatal Abductions

~~*~~

The helicopter flew low along the road toward the ghost town. It was about another twenty miles to the area and Warren was complaining about the lack of anything helpful in the case.

"What do we have so far? Nothing. We've barely seen this thing at night and caught one of their men until he blew his brains out. So far they've taken five people and one agent and we got nothing. I'm not happy," he said.

"When are you ever happy?" Dave said.

Harris yelled back to the men, "We're coming up to the town."

In the distance they could see about five buildings looking weathered grey and worn down. Boards missing in the walls, and windows long gone. There was no activity in the area, and the chopper landed just outside the so called town. The buildings had been erected next to a very steep wall of rock that was a side of a mountain rising up about a dozen yards. The men exited the chopper and walked to the first building. To the right in the wall of mountain was an opening boarded up with warning signs to keep out. Rail tracks entered the opening which was covered by the boards.

Walt, Harris, Sam and Virgil went towards the first building as Warren and Dave went to the boarded up opening in the wall.

"Want to dig for gold?" Dave asked Warren.

"I'll let you do the digging." Warren laughed as he pulled at the boards closing the mine shaft. They didn't move no matter how hard he pulled. "I guess they didn't go through here."

Warren and Dave studied the opening and saw no way in. The tracks went under the boards and they couldn't see much in the dark tunnel through the small openings between the boards. They turned and went back to the first building where the others had gone to.

"Walt, are you in here?" Warren yelled into the door of the dilapidated structure.

He heard a voice from the darkness. "In here." They entered the building and found Harris, Sam and Virgil standing in a room, looking up at Walt who stood on a chair.

"What are you doing up there?" Warren asked.

"I feel air coming out of this opening," he said pointing to an opening in the wall, high up.

"Why would air be coming out of that?" Dave asked.

"That's what I was wondering. I saw dust coming out from this opening. I figured something was up."

Warren went around to the other side of the wall where the opening was coming from. "This is an awfully wide wall. There must be a shaft going down to let the air out. Dave, come here."

Dave went into the other room where Warren was and asked, "What do you want?"

"Help me pull these boards out. There has to be some place that the air is coming from," Warren said.

They pulled on the boards of the wall and finally moved enough to see a metal shaft going up the inside of the wall. "Now this couldn't have been made years ago. Something is below us."

*

Chapter 17

"Maybe Sarah was right. The blimp is in the mountain," Warren said.

"Then what's below us?" Dave asked.

"Maybe their caves. They could be mole people who have never seen the sun." Warren laughed and looked around the room. "See if you can find an opening that may go into the depths of moleville."

"What makes you think it would even be in this building? It could be in any of the seven or so buildings. Or even a secret door in the side of the mountain," Dave said.

"Then we have a lot of exploring to do, don't we?" Warren smiled and continued to nose around. "Walt, come in here and don't fall off the chair."

They heard a crash then Walt yelled, "I'm okay."

Warren and Dave tried not to laugh out loud as Walt limped in the room with the others.

Warren pointed to the shaft. "That wasn't put there when this town was built. So let's see if we can find an opening going below us."

Walt said, "I dropped a small rock down the opening and it took a while before it hit bottom. According to my figures, it's about 80 feet down."

Warren looked at Dave and said, "I hate brainy geeks and their ability to calculate distance with a rock." He turned to the men and told them to split up and search. They left the room as Dave was pulling and tapping on walls.

"I think there would be a bigger opening just to get equipment and supplies into the mountain. If this is a blimp, I'm sure they aren't deflating it and pumping it up to go out every night. Helium is getting harder to obtain from what I hear," Dave said.

Fatal Abductions

"Yeah, children everywhere are mourning the loss of their birthday balloons. If the blimp is somewhere here, it would have to have a huge door to get out of the mountain. Maybe I'll take Harris, have a chopper ride around the mountain top and see if I can find a door opening."

"Don't get shot down. It's a very long walk back to town and I didn't bring my comfortable shoes," Dave said with a smile.

Warren laughed and left the room. Warren found Harris walking around the base of the mountain. "Find anything?" he asked Harris.

"Nope."

"Well, let's look up on top of the mountain and see if we can find an opening for the blimp to exit."

Harris agreed and headed to the chopper. Warren followed closely behind and called Walt on his cell. "I'm taking a chopper ride up top of the mountain to see if there's an opening for the blimp. I'll be back shortly." He hung up and got into the chopper.

Harris took the chopper up and flew over the town so Warren could get a look at the building from the air. He was not seeing any tire tracks from any large vehicles coming or going to the town. This bothered him.

"If they're in this hunk of rock, they're covering their tracks real well," he said to Harris. "Fly along the valley a bit further to see if we can see any tracks."

Harris flew along the valley between the mountains as they watched for tracks. They found nothing all the way up until the valley ended at another mountain wall.

"Dead end. Okay, let's go up top and see what we can find."

Harris flew up and over the crest of the mountain. He slowed around the top as the winds were kicking up, buffeting the chopper slightly.

"Damn, let's not crash, okay?" Warren said, hanging onto the seat with white knuckles.

Harris laughed and flew over the surface of the mountain top. They were watching for any sign of movement from the surface, any scraping on the ground that would signify a big door opening for the blimp. They saw no cracks in the surface that suggested a big door either. They flew around for about twenty minutes.

"Maybe we're spinning our wheels here. It would take years and lots of money to hollow out this mountain to build a blimp base. And building the blimp would put a drain on someone's funds," Harris said.

"I don't see anything here. Let's head back," Warren said.

Harris turned the chopper back toward the town. "Can't you get some fancy equipment from Walt and scan the ground to see if it's hollow?"

Fatal Abductions

Warren gave that thought a bit of attention. "Yeah, I'll ask him when we get back. I'm sure the little genius could come up with a device like that."

Harris hovered over the ground of the town and touched down softly. Warren pulled his hands from their death grip on the seat.

"I never knew you didn't like to fly," Harris said to Warren.

"I'm fine with flying. It's just the landing that bothers me. But you land this thing so well, I'll get used to it." Warren opened the door to get out but turned back to Harris. "You tell anyone I'm afraid of this, I'll see you get assigned to Kuwait." He climbed out and went to Walt standing by.

"Nothing we could see up there. Do you have some machine that can penetrate the ground to see if it's hollow?" Warren said.

"There is a device, but I don't have it with me. I'll call back to the bureau and have it flown out," Walt replied.

"Do it, and put a rush on it. ASAP. We don't know how much time before this thing rises again. Or even if it is here in this area," Warren said to the younger agent.

"Why don't we just camp out here, wait till night and see if it comes out from here?" Dave asked.

Warren thought on that for a moment. "That's not a bad idea. Plus you have the tower spotters, so if we are wrong and this thing isn't here, we can rush to wherever it is." Warren turned to Harris. "Take Walt back to the house to get any equipment or supplies he'll need to help spot the blimp and come right back. It's too creepy out here to be left alone for very long without transportation." He turned back to Walt. "Let everyone know what we have planned. We still have the missiles, but throw in as much weaponry as you can carry."

Walt agreed and went off with Harris. Dave told Virgil to go with them to help. The chopper lifted off and headed back to the house.

"I guess we'll just continue looking around," Warren said. They went off searching again.

About an hour later the chopper returned. Walt and Virgil were pulling things out as Warren, Dave, and Sam came up.

Walt handed Dave a large cooler and said, "Sarah packed a bunch of food for us. Then she pulled out some sleeping bags and air mattresses. You have a lot of camping gear, don't you?"

"I like being ready for anything," Dave said with a grin as he piled up the sleeping equipment next to the cooler. "We'll need some wood to make a fire if we want to stay warm. It gets cold up here at night."

"I'll gather the wood," Sam offered. "I may as well be useful."

"Are we going to sleep by the fire or in one of the buildings? Being in a building will give us more cover in case someone decides to come around with guns," Virgil said.

"That's very true, Virg. Good thinking," Dave said and turned to Warren who was digging around in the cooler.

"Sarah didn't pack any beer," Warren said with a grin. "But there is some good stuff in here to get us through the night."

"Did you hear Virgil?" Dave asked.

"I did, and I think he's right. If these people are crazy enough to kidnap, they could be dangerous. We'll camp out in two buildings so we can cover each other. We'll divide up and that way one group can help the other in case of sneak attack," Warren said.

They spent some time getting ready for the night. "You know if we have to leave here in the night to go somewhere else to chase this thing, we'll have to leave this stuff here," Virgil said.

"We can come back for it later. Or are you worried someone will steal the stuff?" Dave asked his deputy.

"Not that there's anything very important, but it would be bad if you lost your stuff to tourists coming out here."

"Virg, I don't think anyone drives 80 miles from the nearest town to sight-see this place at night. We'll come back in the morning and pick everything up if we have to leave the area tonight."

"Works for me, I guess," Virgil said and went out of the building they chose to camp out in. It was in sight of the other building where the others would be staying.

"We'll have to take shifts of two men to watch for the blimp to go up, if it does," Warren said to Dave.

"One man from each building so they can go wake the others," Dave replied.

"Right. Walt brought back the radios for the tower spotters. Give them a call and see if they'll work in this valley."

Dave took the radios out of the building and made a call. He reached Otis, one of the spotters, and told him he was checking the radio. It worked fine, said Otis.

"Be alert for the object in the sky. Call us immediately if you see it," Dave said, signed off and went back in the building to report to Warren.

Virgil yelled to Dave, "We got company." Dave stuck his head out the door as Virgil pointed down the road where a pick-up truck was approaching.

Warren came out of the building and went to Dave. The pick-up truck came up and stopped. Two very big men got out and stood by the truck.

"They don't look like aliens," Virgil said.

*

Chapter 18

The passenger of the truck reached back in and came out with a rifle. The driver just stood then yelled, "This is private property, you'll need to leave now!" The passenger raised his rifle slightly towards the men.

From their left Walt, Harris and Sam came out of their building carrying large automatic weapons pointed at the two men.

"I'd say you are out powered. If you want to start something, go ahead," Warren called to them. He drew out his service pistol as did Dave and aimed them at the men.

The two of them looked stunned. The passenger lowered the rifle and then held it by the barrel.

Warren and Dave went to the men as the others gathered behind them. Dave went forward and said, "See this badge? I'm Sheriff Chandler of the Jefferson County Sheriff's Department. This man behind me is an agent of the FBI as are the others. Now maybe you want to tell us how you figure this is private property?"

They didn't say anything. Warren told them to come around the front of the truck and put their hands on the hood of the truck. They did it slowly. Dave took the rifle from the passenger and handed it to Virgil. The men assumed the position as Warren frisked them.

"Okay, turn around," Warren said. They did.

"Now the sheriff asked you a question. Who owns this property if it's so private that you have to threaten us to get lost?"

The men didn't say anything again. "Damn, did they cut out your tongues too?" Warren said.

Both men looked surprised.

"Ah, that hit a nerve. Do you miss you friend Sergio? He blew his brains out in our office," Warren said.

The men now looked curious. The passenger glanced at the driver and said, "Sergio is dead?"

The driver said, "Shut up, fool." He looked back at Warren and said, "Why did you kill our cook?"

"We didn't. He killed himself rather than tell us who he worked for. But I'm sure you can tell us that now, and we won't let you kill yourselves," Warren replied.

They were silent again. "Your boss must be a pretty mean man to prevent you from talking, tongue or not." He looked at Walt and told him, "You and Harris handcuff these men. Suspicion of fraud in regards to the property for starters, and threatening the lives of Federal agents."

They restrained the two men and pushed them towards one of the buildings. "Secure them good. I don't want them running off to their employer and blabbing," Warren said.

Fatal Abductions

They took the men into the building as Warren turned to Dave.

"I don't think they'll tell us anything. Unless you want to beat the crap out of them?" Warren said.

"No, I'm a pacifist. But thanks for the offer." Dave grinned. "You're more sadistic than me."

"Well, let's see what the truck tells us." He turned to the vehicle and went to it. Dave went around to the driver's side and checked the visor for a registration. He studied it and said, "It's registered to a company called V-SOC, Inc. I've never heard of them around here."

"I'll have Walt run a check on them when he gets back from making our guests comfortable. This truck is relatively clean," he said, looking under the seats.

He went to the bed of the truck and pulled a tarp back. Under it were two 50 gallon barrels lying on their sides. There were hoses coming from them like you'd find in a gas station. Warren lifted one hose and smelled the end by the handle.

"Wow, that's strange stuff. Not gas but different, more like kerosene," he said.

Dave came around and Warren held the hose for him to smell. "I've smelled that when I was in the Army. It's rocket fuel. For jet engines, if I remember correctly, I think it's called JP-4. JP for jet propellant. It's a mixture of gasoline and kerosene. Now what would our guest be doing with jet fuel?"

"Shall we douse them in it and hold a match till they tell us?" Warren laughed.

"I like the idea, but let's do it the old fashioned way first. Beat them senseless."

"You're losing your pacifist status." Warren put the handle back down then looked around more. There were various tools and what looked like machine parts. "Recognize any of these, Mr. Rocketman?"

"Nope, they're strange to me. A lot like you." He turned and went to the other side of the truck bed. He reached in and opened a long thin box. "Well, this is interesting," he said bringing out a rocket launcher.

Warren came around and took the launcher from Dave. He held it on his shoulder and aimed it at a building on the end of the town. He pulled the trigger and a rocket exploded out the front end and blew up the building.

"Shit, I didn't know it was loaded," Warren said in shock. "I hope none of the men were in that building."

Everyone came running out from wherever they were and looked at the building now burning in rubble. Warren took a head count and everyone was present. He breathed a sigh of relief and put the launcher back in Dave's hands. "He did it!" Warren yelled to the men.

Dave just said, "Ass," and handed it back to Warren. "They wanted to be prepared for something big with this thing."

Fatal Abductions

Warren saw a couple more rockets. "Anyone knows how to load this thing?" he asked as the other men came up.

Sam laughed and said, "That's an RPG or Rocket-propelled Grenade launcher. They were big back in 1957 or so. We called them Bazookas, anti-tank weapons. Yeah, it's not hard to load." He went to the truck, brought out one of the rockets and proceeded to load the thing. "I was a grunt in infantry. I used a few of these."

"Good. You're now in charge of it. Don't blow anyone up," Warren told the man. "Did you have anything to do with jet fuel, too?"

"After I got out of the infantry, I became a helicopter pilot. Yes, I was involved with all types of fuels. Why?" Sam asked.

Warren pointed to the barrels. "What do you make of them having that stuff? Dave said it was JC-4."

JP-4," Dave corrected.

"Wow, JP-4, that's old school jet fuel. These guys must have bought all this stuff at an army surplus store," Sam said.

"It's going to be dark soon, let's finish getting our areas set up," Warren said.

"What if someone misses the two men? They may come looking for them," Virgil said.

"True. How did they know we were here? Did they just come back from somewhere and find us, or did they spot us from their base? I don't see any spy cameras around," Warren said.

"I think they were coming back from town and found us. I hope that's the right explanation. Otherwise they'll send more men out to bother us," Dave said.

"If they didn't know we were here, then where were they heading? There has to be an opening here somewhere that they were going to," Walt said.

"You got it, little buddy. We need to continue to find that opening. We may need the bazooka to blow open the door," Warren said.

"Say, was there a garage door opener in the truck? They'd need some way to open a secret door," Virgil said.

Warren smiled and went to the truck, looking around the cab. He didn't find anything resembling a wireless opener. "Nope, nothing. Maybe they'd call from a cell phone and have someone open the door. Did you search the men in the building, Walt?"

"Yes, and they both had cell phones," he said.

"I want to see those phones. We may be able to track their calls and see who they talked to. Oh, and I need you to check on a company called V-SOC, Inc."

Walt said he would and pulled out his cell phone. Warren and Dave headed to the building where the men were tied up. Warren yelled back to the men and told them to finish getting the equipment ready.

Warren and Dave went into the building where they found the men still handcuffed together on the floor, back to back. They were now tied together by rope they found in the building.

Warren stooped down and said, "I'm sorry but we used one of your rockets. I'll see if we can replace it for you. I think I may blow up this building next, if you don't mind. And you'll be in it." He smiled and flicked the ear of the driver.

"Ow, you can't do that!" the man protested.

"I can do anything I want. After we blow you up, you won't be able to complain to anyone, will you?"

The driver was silent. Warren got up and went to a table where Walt had put their personal items. He opened the wallets, studied the faces in the pictures and said, "Well, Boris, that sounds like a Russian name. You Russian?"

The driver said nothing. "Okay, be that way again. I guess you two will be useless to us. So we don't need you. Back when I worked with a special group of soldiers in South America, they had a saying. 'Take no prisoners.'"

Warren picked up the personal items and headed to the door. Dave followed, looking at the men still on the floor. "My friend is crazy and I'm sure he doesn't want to drag you two around."

The men said nothing. They sat there as Warren and Dave went out. After a few minutes they heard something that chilled them.

It was Warren yelling from outside, "Fire in the hole!"

*

Chapter 19

Warren was standing next to Sam with the bazooka aimed at the property next to the building that held the two men. "Go ahead and fire close, but don't hit the building," Warren told Sam.

Sam fired the weapon and hit the ground about twenty feet from the building. The explosion shook the ground fiercely. Warren went to the window of the building where he could see the men lying on their sides, squirming to get loose.

Warren poked his head into the window and said, "Sorry, I missed the building. I'm not real good with this thing. But I'll try it again. I'll get it right this time. Nice knowing you."

He backed away from the window and waited. The men were screaming something Warren couldn't understand. It sounded like Russian or German. Then they spoke English.

141

Fatal Abductions

"All right! All right! We'll talk, don't shoot!" one of them was yelling.

Warren waited then went back to Sam and said to fire on the other side of the building. He did, this time a bit closer. It blew out one side of the building but not where the men were. The men were really screaming now.

Warren turned to Dave and said, "Shall we go see what our guests want? They should be real ready to talk now."

Warren, Dave, Walt and Virgil went into the building. Walt and Virgil pulled the men up and sat them on a chair. They had half a seat each and looked scared.

"Now I need some answers. Who do you work for?" Warren asked.

"We don't know the people who run the thing. We're just workers in the factory making the parts for the machine they have."

"What machine?"

"I haven't seen it but they say it's big and dangerous. They plan to use it to take over the United States."

Warren looked at Dave then said, "Where is this machine?"

"We don't know that either. They have many workers, but each of us doesn't know what the others are doing. That way we don't know everything. They are very secretive."

Walt said, "The same way the pyramids were built. They had different people working on different areas, then they killed them to be sure no one knew how to enter into the center of the pyramids."

"Clever. Okay, where is the opening to the area you work in?" Warren turned back to the men.

They were silent again. "Sam, get the bazooka ready. This time I won't miss."

He was heading to the door when Boris said, "It's in the mine shaft."

"We checked that. The opening is sealed and it goes nowhere," Warren said.

"It opens when I dial a number on my phone."

Warren pulled the cell phone out of his pocket. He checked the phone calls and found about a dozen of the same number. He turned to his men. "Let's see if we can open the magic door."

They left the building and walked to the mine shaft opening. Warren looked the boards over and said, "I don't see how this thing opens. But here it goes." He hit the redial and waited.

Suddenly there was a rumble and the boards moved out and upward on very large steel arms. The tunnel was reinforced with metal walls and ceiling. The rail tracks stopped just inside the opening and there were hoses on the bottom of the board door.

Fatal Abductions

Warren hit the speed dial again and as the door moved to close the hoses spewed out high pressure air to the ground, blowing away any possible tire prints.

"That's why there are no tire tracks. They obliterated them. Clever. I think before we go doing something stupid like going into the depths of hell, we need back up. Walt, call the field director and get us some more men."

"They won't get here until tomorrow. When I called for our extra men I was told this," Walt said.

Warren looked at Harris. "Get in the chopper, go back and get the rest of the men back in Brinnon. We'll wait for you."

Harris ran off to the chopper and was in the air quickly. They watched as he went off.

~~*~~

"We were guinea pigs to see if we could escape. Why?" Michaels asked the men standing in a new cell. This one had bars.

"Guess it was to test their security, maybe," George said.

"They didn't even have guards. What were we supposed to do, stand around until we were caught? They had to be watching us all this time."

Steve said, "Psychological testing. To see if we are good enough to get by their security. Maybe that's why they chose us. We each have a different set of skills. George was good at escaping his captors in the war. You're a Federal agent, I'm a cop and Jack is a car thief. Even he has skills."

"Very good, Mr. Goodwin," came a voice from outside the cell. "That's what we were doing. Testing our security. We have very special guests that will be joining us and we want to be sure they don't escape either." A light came on and the man in the formal uniform came forward from a dark corner. As he got closer the prisoners could see his uniform better. It was a Nazi uniform, right out of the Third Reich.

"Son of a bitch. You're a damn Nazi." Jack spit at him, but the man was too far to hit.

"Neo-Nazi, please. We take pride in our heritage, but we will do better than the Reich did. We are part of a bigger picture. There are more parts to this than you can imagine. We are an army of soldiers now, and our job is to protect the others who will be doing the big picture."

"What? Are you trying to take over the world again?" Steve asked.

"This time we are riding along with a higher authority and will start with the United States. Once they take over this country, we'll be able to either have other countries come under their regime or we'll destroy them."

Fatal Abductions

"You're talking about World War Three. The last one. Every country with a bomb will be fighting you and there will be no world to take over," Michaels said.

"We won't need bombs. We have a bigger weapon that will give us superiority over the others. Their bombs will be useless. But you gentlemen will have no worries about that. You'll be dead."

~~*~~

The chopper arrived back in the town with the five agents who came out from Seattle to help. Warren went to greet them and explain what they had to do.

"So that's the plan. We go into the hole until we find something. Everyone load up on weapons. I have no idea what we'll find and I don't want us to be caught with our pants down."

The men agreed and went to get the weapons from the chopper.

"Are you comfortable going into the hole?" Dave asked Warren. "I know you are not happy with enclosed places."

"I'll be fine as long as we keep moving. I'm sure we'll find a bigger area where they are working. We just have to be quick and quiet," Warren said.

"Okay, I'll be behind you to push," Dave said with a grin.

Everyone gathered at the mine shaft and waited while Warren dialed the number. The door slid open and the men rushed in following Warren. Every ten yards they progressed, a light came on to light the way.

"This tunnel is big enough to fit a pick-up truck, but nothing more. I wonder if they have a bigger opening to take things out bigger than a bread box," Warren said quietly. After a while and what seemed to be another mile of walking, they started to hear movement and noises. Warren held his hand up and everyone stopped.

"Okay, be on your toes. Dave and I will go first to see what we can see, then we'll call you," he said to the agents, pilots, Virgil and Walt.

He and Dave moved close along the wall towards the area that was getting lighter. They came to an opening into a much larger room where there were a number of trucks and jeeps and about three men working on the vehicles.

"I wonder if our missing jeep is here," Dave said.

"This seems to be a motor pool, judging by all the vehicles. There's a couple doors going out to somewhere." He moved out in the opening and spoke out loud. "Hey guys, our truck broke down in the tunnel. Can you help?"

The three men looked up, grabbed guns and ran towards the opening.

Fatal Abductions

"Oops, I guess that did it," Warren said to Dave as they ran back to the others.

The men entered the tunnel and ran after Dave and Warren until they came to a wall of agents all aiming automatic weapons at them.

"Guys, I would suggest you drop the guns. You're sort of outnumbered," Warren said to the now surprised men.

They went to the men and took their weapons. Two of the agents wrapped their wrists in wire ties. Then they put the restraints on their ankles. They left the men on the floor of the tunnel.

They cautiously went into the open area and walked between the vehicles towards the doors. They went through the closest door and found it went into a hallway. Carefully they opened another door and found a large lab with men working at a big machine hanging in the middle of the room.

"That thing looks like a weapon. Do we really want to know what it is?" Warren said.

*

Chapter 20

Every one of the men gathered by the door as Warren walked in like he belonged there. He had already told Dave that the men looked more like scientists than hoods so they shouldn't have any problems.

A few of the men looked curiously at Warren and then ignored him. He walked up to the hanging machine and said to the nearest man, "So is it about ready to go?"

The man gave Warren a stare and asked, "Who are you?"

"I'm the new supervisor for operations. Now answer my question."

The man was silent then said, "We have about two more days, then it will be ready."

"Are you going to test it and where?" Warren was playing it up, not knowing what to say.

The man stared again and said, "Do you know what this is?"

Warren didn't know what to say. "I don't need to know. I just have to know you're ready to go. Now are you?"

The man said, "I'm not sure if I should talk to you. I need to talk to our supervisor." He started to walk away

Fatal Abductions

when Warren grabbed him, swung him around and put his service pistol into his face.

"Okay, I'll stop being nice." Warren yelled to his men and they came in with weapons ready. The other five people in the room were gathered and bound by the wrists.

Warren was still holding the man and sat him down on a chair, his gun still in his face.

"Talk to me or I'll shoot you. I'll say you tried to escape. Nice and simple."

The man looked tired. "Will you get me out of this place and away from these people?"

"What's wrong with these people?" Warren asked. "And who are these people?"

The man was silent. Warren burst out, "I'm tired of everyone not talking. You talk to me and I'll spare you. If you don't, I'll shoot your ass. Now talk!"

The man looked startled and said, "We were hired because we knew about the old secret Vril Society and their claim to a power that would be able to make objects fly and destroy countries."

"Huh?" Warren said and looked at Walt. "Do you know what he's talking about?"

Walt came close and said, "It was made famous by an author named Edward Bulwer-Lytton. He published a science fiction novel, 'The Power of the Coming Race,' which describes an underground race of angel-like superhuman creatures and their mysterious energy force, the Vril, an 'all-permeating fluid' of limitless power. The Nazis and Hitler tried to harness this power but didn't succeed. I guess someone didn't give up on the whole theory."

"Great, we have a secret society associated with Hitler and they want to take over the world." He looked at the man still cowering. "Is that what they're doing?"

"That's their intent. But it's all a lot of bull and we are playing along with them to keep from being killed. That thing hanging there is what the Nazis built during the war to further their attempt to rule the world based on flawed theory."

"Are you telling me these people can build underground bases and fly a huge blimp to kidnap people and they don't know this stuff won't work?" Warren asked.

"Blimp? What blimp?" the man asked.

Warren stared at the man and then said, "You don't know about the blimp? Okay, do you know about a flying saucer or machine that can fly in and grab up people from the ground?"

The man looked confused and said, "I know of no machine they have. We've been in here for about a year and I haven't any idea what is going on in the world. No TV or outside communications."

"Wow, you have a lot of catching up to do. You don't even know who the Kardashians are, do you?" Warren said.

Fatal Abductions

"Who?" he said.

"My point exactly, but you aren't missing anything." Warren turned to Walt and said, "Take these people out of here, bind them for pick up and call for back up. Tell the director we have a big situation here. Terrorism at its finest."

Walt and two agents gathered the men and took them out. Warren went to the machine hanging from the ceiling by chains. "This thing is supposed to help rule the world?"

Dave came up and said, "I wouldn't touch it. It could be dangerous."

"I'm no fool. I'm not going to even breathe on it." He backed away from it and turned to Dave. "I'm concerned."

"That we haven't been stopped by whoever runs this place? I was wondering too," Dave said.

"I would imagine that they'd have guards all over the place to protect this amazing weapon. If it is amazing."

"Or maybe the people in charge know it isn't amazing. This place could be a front. To draw us away from the real base," Dave said.

"Boy, you are good at this investigating stuff. I like your theories. Shall we explore the rest of the base?" Warren said and headed to the door. Dave followed.

Warren pulled out his cell and called Walt. "Get someone to pick up our prisoners and get back down here. Bring some of your equipment to tell us if we're dealing with any radioactive crap." He hung up. "I'm not taking any chances. Someday I want children."

"Your own? That I want to see." Dave laughed. "Okay shall we go out and wait for Walt?"

They left the lab and the hanging device. They waited outside the door until Walt came running up, breathless.

"Walt, take it easy, you'll get a heart attack," Warren said to his partner.

They turned to the other door and went to it. This door was further away from the lab so they figured there would be something else behind it. Maybe offices.

They approached the door and Warren opened it. There was a room and it looked like quarters for the lab men. There were bunk beds and tables, a row of lockers on one wall and a bathroom to the left. The men walked around examining the quarters.

"Spending a year in this place would be a real fun prison. I feel sorry for the men who had to endure this," Warren said.

"Well, you found your mole people," Dave said and left the room.

Walt and Warren followed him and they stood looking around the hallway. There were no other doors going anywhere, just the lab and the quarters.

Fatal Abductions

"Okay, we have a motor pool and then a lab next to their quarters. Where do the workers go to make parts, as the men in the truck said?" Dave asked.

"Geez, do I have to actually blow up the building to get them to talk? I think we were set up. This whole thing is a sham. While we waste time here the real criminals are out flying around grabbing people."

"You think the workers in the lab were in on the sham?" Walt asked.

"I guess we'll put them in the building and blow them up too. What do I have to do to get people to talk?"

They went back out to the motor pool and opened the second door. It was a kitchen. "Well, we know where the cook was heading with the groceries."

They couldn't find any other areas in the base and Warren was getting frustrated. They went back to the surface and it was going to get dark soon.

Warren went to the lab men, now sitting in the same building with the men from the truck. He stood looking at all of them then blew up like a crazy person.

"What the hell are you all trying to pull?" He stomped around and then said, "Somebody tell me what the hell this underground base is for, and I want the truth!"

He drew his weapon and fired it to the floor between the truck men and the lab men. Everyone flinched. He went to the head lab man and pulled him up. Warren took the man out of the building.

They were gone for a few seconds. Walt and Dave were in the room waiting when they heard a gunshot. Warren came back in and yelled, "I don't like lies! Now who is next to be shot in the head?" He went to one of the truck men and pulled him up. The man looked terrified as Warren dragged him out of the building. Dave was trying not to laugh.

About two minutes later, another gunshot. Warren stormed back in. "As long as I have ammo, I'll shoot every one of you until I get a real answer."

The men were looking frightened, which was what Warren was trying to accomplish. He went to a man who looked to him to be the most frightened and pulled him up.

"NO! Don't kill me, please," the man wailed.

Warren dragged the man out still screaming. Dave followed them out as Warren took the man to a chair on the road and sat him down with his back to the other two men Warren had taken out earlier. They were sitting on the ground across the yard by another building being guarded by Warren's men.

"Okay, talk to me, asswipe. What is this base for?"

"It's a diversion. We've been in there waiting for anyone to find us," the man said, nearly crying.

"So you aren't working on a weapon?" Warren asked into his face.

"We don't have the weapon here, it's in another base. I don't know where. Honestly, please believe me," he said, watching Warren bring up his gun.

"Who's behind this?" Warren asked.

"Mark told you the truth. It's the Vril Society. We are here to be a distraction. They took the agent's tracker from him and led you here by that. They have a very close time table for getting the ship running properly to capture the President."

Warren stared at the man and said, "President? Of the United States?"

*

Chapter 21

"Yes, the president is coming to Seattle tomorrow to help some senator get re-elected. They're going to grab him when he's outside talking at a rally."

"Do these nutcases think they can just grab the man and get away?" Warren said.

"Who's going to shoot down an airship with the president aboard?" the man said.

Warren looked at Dave. "He's right. They won't endanger POTUS. If they can grab him, they could get away with it. I need to call Seattle. Watch him," he said to Walt and went off to make a call.

Dave followed him and stopped him before he could call. "Warren, how are they going to fly over and grab the president? He'll have Secret Service all around him. We now know it's some person who comes down from the blimp and grabs the subject. They would shoot him before he could get to POTUS."

"They would have to cause some diversion, I would imagine to give them time to grab the man," Warren said.

"I would imagine if some huge flying machine suddenly came over the president, they'd take him away from the site quickly," Dave said.

"Well, they have something planned. I have to warn them. He pulled his cell phone out and placed the call. "What the hell? My phone isn't working."

Dave pulled his phone out and got the same result. "They must be blocking the phones somehow."

"Who? We have all the men captive, so who's blocking us?" Warren asked.

"Maybe some room we missed with people who are watching us," Dave said.

"Well, let's get Harris, fly back to town and call. They couldn't block us from there."

Warren called to Harris who was helping to guard the two men Warren pretended to shoot. He came over and

Fatal Abductions

Warren explained what he needed. He went to Walt and also explained.

"Let me try my phone," Walt said. He pulled his phone out and tried but got nothing. "This has to be deliberate. These mountains didn't block my calls before."

"Okay, that's enough for me. I'm flying back with Harris to call as soon as we are out of range of this place." Warren went to the chopper where Dave and Harris were waiting for him. They got in and Harris tried to start the chopper, but it just sat there, doing nothing.

"What is this?" Warren exploded when Harris said it wouldn't start. "See what's wrong with the damn thing. We need to get out of here fast." Harris did his best to get the chopper to start but couldn't. He got out and checked the engine.

"Warren, someone pulled wires on the thing," Harris said, showing him the few loose wires.

"Sabotage?" he yelled. "Someone we haven't caught is loose and doing this."

"Or it could be one of your own men," Dave said, getting out of the chopper.

"My own agents? Never. They have all been carefully screened and check out before we even let them in the field. But if I find out it is one of them, I'll strangle them myself." He stomped around the chopper thinking. "How do we get word back to the bureau to warn the secret service about the possible attack on the president?"

Harris tried his radio in the chopper and said it wouldn't work. Dave tried the radios to the towers and they were useless. "There's something blocking transmissions," Dave said.

Warren was looking at the cliffs around them. "Maybe we can climb up and get past the blockage."

Dave said, "It's worth a try."

Warren called Sam over. "Sam, you and Walt see if you can get up the side of this hill and call back to Seattle. Maybe the phone block is just down here. They couldn't possibly blank the whole area."

Sam and Walt grabbed radios and cell phones and went to a trail that they hoped would lead up. Warren turned to Dave. "If they can't get through, we have a problem. I'm not walking 80 miles to town."

"Maybe if we walked a couple miles down the road, we might get out of the area being blocked."

Warren stared at Dave, then he went to the pick-up truck sitting by. He got in and tried to start it. It was also dead. "Okay, I can do a couple miles." He yelled to the remaining agents to gather. The prisoners were all bound so they wouldn't escape.

"In case you haven't heard, we have no communications to the outside of this valley. Sheriff Chandler and I are going to walk down this road to see if we can get out from under the blockage and call for help. Now, another matter. Someone sabotaged the helicopter and this truck. I expect you agents to act like agents and find out who that person or persons is, who did this. I hope you have this solved by the time I get back. Keep an eye on our prisoners. Now go to it."

The men went back to their prisoners and were talking amongst themselves. Warren turned to Dave and said, "Shall we go hiking?"

They started back down the road, hoping to gain phone access.

"Did Walt ever get through to the bureau about coming to pick up the prisoners?" Dave asked.

Warren thought on it and said, "I told him to do that, but I didn't ask if he did. He would have told me if he couldn't have gotten word to them, so maybe we have help coming. I can't call Walt to ask." Warren stopped and looked up the side of the mountain where Sam and Walt went. "I don't see them. Let's do this quickly so we can get back to see if they had any luck."

They walked for about twenty minutes. "I'm ready to retire," Warren said abruptly. "I've had enough chasing criminals and now world conquering nutjobs. I think I'd like to move to your neck of the woods and fish the canal every day."

Dave laughed and said, "You'd drown yourself after a month, you'd get so bored. Ever since I've known you, you've thrived on this. I can't see you retiring unless you were seriously wounded."

"That's another thing I'm concerned about. I've come very close to being shot a number of times. How many more bullets can I dodge before one finds its way to my vital organs?"

"So wear your vest," Dave said.

"You know that thing is heavy and bulky. I wish they'd create a nice seersucker three piece suit that's impervious to bullets. With a thin pin striping, dark blue. Tailored to fit."

Dave smiled and said, "You don't ask for much, do you? Think you'll ever decide to find a woman who can keep up with you?"

"I already told you that you have the woman I want. I may shoot you out here, bury your body and go comfort the widow."

"That's the only way you could comfort her. Sarah said she'd look around for a female for you."

"Great. Some backwoods woman with gaps in her teeth and scraggly hair." Warren laughed as they walked.

"I don't think Sarah knows anyone who fits that description. But she does have a few attractive friends. One that I know who I try not to stare too hard at when she's around. Sarah laughs at my restraint."

Warren stopped and said, "I think we've gone far enough." He pulled his cell phone out and pushed buttons, then listened. "Crap, it's still not working. What did they do, blow up a cell tower?"

Fatal Abductions

Dave tried his phone and got the same result. "How far do you think we've gone?"

Warren looked around and said, "The bureau doesn't teach how to judge mileage. Just how to report mileage for our vehicles. We usually make that up."

They were standing in the road when they heard a noise coming. "I think we have a vehicle coming," Warren said. They waited until the truck came in view.

"Think he'll stop for us?" Dave asked.

"If not, we'll shoot him. Besides, where is he going? He has to be going to our fake base."

They waited until the truck got closer and Warren stood in the middle of the road, waving his arms. The truck slowed then sped up, directly at Warren. Dave pulled his gun and aimed it at the single occupant of the truck. Warren had his weapon out and fired at the passenger side of the truck, not wanting to hit the driver. The windshield shattered on that side and the driver drove off the side of the road and stopped quickly.

The man got out of the truck and started firing a gun at the men. Dave and Warren had no cover to go to, so they just fired back. The man was behind the truck door covering him. Dave aimed at the man's legs and hit him. The man screamed and collapsed, still holding on to the door. Warren ran, pushed the door into the man and held his gun at the man's head.

"Please give me a reason to shoot you! All we need is your truck," Warren yelled at the man.

Dave came up and grabbed the gun from the man's hand being held between the door and the truck body. Warren released the door and pulled the man out of the truck. The man fell to the ground holding his leg.

"Good shot, Dave," Warren said.

"Lots of practice shooting trees," Dave said with a smile.

Warren leaned down to the man and said, "We can leave you out here to die or you can get in the back of the truck and be nice. We'll take you to your base and get your leg taken care of."

The man mumbled, "I'll take the truck bed."

*

Chapter 22

They put the man in the truck bed and tied him up with rope they found in the back. Warren jumped in the cab and started the truck back up. Dave got in and they rode back to the town.

As they pulled up they saw that the agents had all of the prisoners in the center of the town sitting on the ground. Warren parked as Walt came up.

Fatal Abductions

"We couldn't get a signal as far up as we could go. They must have some powerful jamming device around here. We couldn't get anyone to talk, but I don't think they even know what's going on. They're just stooges to waste our time," Walt explained.

"It's okay. We have a truck now and I'm going back to call Seattle to warn them and have everyone here picked up. Walt, you come with us. You can bring the van back here to help figure this place out." He turned to his agents and said, "Keep an eye out in case anyone else rides in. The guy in the back was armed. Harris, I'll have someone bring parts out to get the chopper running."

Warren had the man taken out of the truck bed and told Sam to get his first-aid kit and patch the guy's leg.

Warren told Dave, "Time's a-wasting. Shall we go?"

They got back in the truck and drove out.

On the road, Walt said, "We did a search of the buildings and the underground base and could find no equipment that could jam our phones and radios. There must be something on top of the mountain that's doing this."

"Doesn't matter now, Walt We have transportation back to where we can call. Keep trying your phone and tell me when we are out of range for the jammer."

They drove on for about a half hour and Walt said he still couldn't get through.

"This is strange. We are about thirty miles from the town. Is there any jammer that can reach this far?" Warren asked Walt.

"Not that I know of. The only other thing I can think is they did something to the cell towers. That would cut off all communications between here and Seattle."

"Then that's what we have to consider. If we don't warn the secret service then the bad guys could carry out their plan," Warren said.

Dave listened to the men and said, "If they knocked out the cell towers, then how did they prevent the radios from working?"

"Don't you have some easy questions to ask?" Warren said. "Walt, can you answer the man?"

"Unfortunately, I don't have an answer for that," Walt said. "Unless they have some powerful EMF projecting device that would disrupt radio transmissions. That could be a source. If so, we are dealing with some pretty sophisticated equipment."

Warren smiled at Dave and said, "Did that answer your question?"

"Keep your eyes on the road, please," Dave said back to him.

They drove on for another hour and were almost in sight of Brinnon. "This would have been so much faster with the chopper. We have two now and both don't work. This is getting out of hand," Warren said.

Fatal Abductions

"Well, shortly we'll be able to do something about it," Dave said hopefully.

"I'm not holding my breath. We've had too many problems with this whole situation. I'm wondering if this Vril whatever is more clever than we give them credit for."

"How are we going to communicate if radios here won't work? My cell is still blocked," Walt said.

Dave said, "We'll try Mike's shortwave ham radio in the station and see if we can get through."

"Good. Shortwave uses a different frequency than the radios. It just may work," Walt said.

They approached the station and saw a bunch of cars out front. "Crap, everyone is probably bitching about lack of telephone service. I hope Mike is holding up."

They parked out front and went in. The group of people standing at the counter saw Dave and surrounded him with questions. "Okay, everyone shut up or I'll have you all ejected from the building. We have a dangerous situation and we need to do something about it. Now go home or to work and wait. I'll try and get to the bottom of the phone problem. You can't help the situation by clogging up the office. Now leave, please."

They all mumbled but left. After the room was clear, Dave went to Mike and said, "Fire up your shortwave and see if you can hook up to anyone in Seattle."

Mike went to the radio he had set up in the corner of the office and flipped switches. Dave turned to Warren and said, "Mike's hobby is communicating with the world. I let him set up one of his radios here so he could keep himself out of trouble."

Mike was busy wanting to get through to anyone, but couldn't. "Damn, there's something interfering with the transmission. Has to be sunspots."

"Or a big enough pulsar wave created by someone locally. I don't understand why they are singling us out," Walt said.

"They came out here to grab up a few more people. They knew we'd call the FBI in and then investigate. So they led us astray with this very clever ruse," Dave said. "They went to a lot of trouble for this."

"Who knows, they may have other places set up just like this," Warren said.

"But there were no reports of abductions by alien craft anywhere else. Since the president is coming here, they're giving their attentions to this area," Walt said.

"They had this planned for a long while. It took time to build those rooms underground. And how would they know long ago just when they could grab the president over in Seattle?"

"Maybe that base wasn't a front originally. Maybe they actually did work on their project there and finished it. They left the place as a diversion when they were finished," Warren said.

167

Fatal Abductions

"As good a theory as any. So we need to drive back to Seattle to warn them of the kidnap attempt on POTUS. The way you drive we will be there in no time," Dave said to Warren. "We can take my Bronco. It's faster than the van. Besides Walt should take it back to the town to see what he can find out."

"I agree. Shall we go to your house and start this?" Warren said.

"Mike, the phones will be out for a while, I figure. So just tell everyone to be patient." Dave went to the TV on the wall and turned it on.

Mike said, "There's nothing. I tried it to see if there was some story on the news about the phone blackout."

"Well, they aren't fooling around, are they?" Warren said. "Let's get moving before the aliens attack. It's getting dark out now, and we don't have a lot of time before the rally in the morning."

They went out to the Bronco and over to Dave's place. They pulled in and Sarah came running out followed by Alex. "Dave, I was so worried when I couldn't reach you. Is everything alright?"

"Not really. We need to get to Seattle quickly. The president is in danger and we have to warn the secret service."

"Oh, is that all? I thought it was something important," Sarah said with a grin.

"Yeah, I'll take care of you when I get back for that smart remark."

"I'll be waiting," she said and kissed him. "Be careful."

"I will. Warren, let's roll," he said, then he and Warren went to his Bronco. Warren had given last minute instructions to Walt as the young agent went to his van.

Everyone drove out of the driveway as Sarah and Alex watched.

"Is it always like this? Being married to a sheriff?" Alex asked her.

"It's always like this," she replied.

Dave was barreling down the 101 with sirens and flashers going. "We have an hour and a half of travel at this rate. So shall we sing some songs?"

"Sure, but no country." Warren started to sing a Beatles song, then Dave reached over and tried the radio. It didn't work.

"Damn, I shouldn't have suggested it," he said quietly.

They were about fifteen minutes out of Seattle when they started to see convoys of military vehicles moving along the road passing them faster than they were traveling.

Fatal Abductions

"What the hell? Where are they going?" Warren asked.

"Try your cell and see if it's working now."

Warren pulled his cell phone, but still got no response. "They must have knocked out the phone towers. I wish I had a satellite phone." They drove on and the roadway was suddenly becoming congested with cars going into the city. Dave still had his flasher going and drove off the road to move on the shoulder. He had to avoid a few irate drivers pulling out on the shoulder to get by.

Dave came up behind them and was honking. They finally pulled off the side of the road to let Dave pass. "There's something going on. Maybe the aliens invaded," Warren said.

"I doubt that. These people aren't aliens. They are misguided fanatics who think they'll take over the country."

"The U.S. has never been invaded by anyone, let alone aliens. There's something wrong here."

They drove on the shoulder for a couple miles as traffic was almost at a standstill. They came up to a makeshift blockade by military vehicles.

Dave pulled up to the soldiers who were waving them over. Dave rolled down his window and yelled to the officer, "What's going on?"

"And you are?" he asked.

Warren had his badge out and yelled, "Federal Agent Stevens, FBI. We're here to warn the secret service that there will be a kidnapping attempt on the president. Let us through."

The officer leaned into the window and said, "Yeah, well you're a little late. The president has already been taken."

*

Chapter 23

Dave gave a shocked look at Warren. Warren leaned further to the window and said, "When did this happen?"

"About two hours ago. Someone grabbed him as he was outside with Senator Gregg. They were touring the downtown area. That's all I know. Are you wanting to go into the city?" the officer asked.

"Why are you stopping people from entering the city?" Warren asked.

"There's some kind of flying ship hovering over the city. We don't know what it wants yet, but we do know the president is aboard. Otherwise we'd blow the damn thing out of the sky."

"Let us pass. I need to get to the bureau."

Fatal Abductions

The officer signaled to the jeep blocking the center of the road and the driver pulled over. Dave thanked the officer and drove through.

"I've been to the bureau only twice, so get me there from here," Dave said to Warren.

Warren guided Dave to the building and he parked out front. They jumped from the Bronco and ran to the door. Warren stopped just outside and looked up. The sky was black, no stars in the bright city. They couldn't see the airship which didn't mean it wasn't up there. They went in.

"Stevens! It's about time you got here. Talk to me!" came a voice from above on the walkway to the second floor. It was the field director.

"We have a long story to tell you. Gather any agent who needs to be updated on the ship above us," Warren said as he and Dave ran up the stairs.

They met in a conference room with all the department heads who were called in when the president was taken. They sat at the huge table as Warren took the head and stood with the director. Everyone was finally seated and Warren started.

"I'm going to try and make this brief, but I have much to tell, so please no questions until I'm finished." He cleared his throat and took a drink of water from the glass in front of him.

He explained the story from when they first saw the machine in the air and what happened for the next two days. He covered the underground base and the people

172

who were there. Then he told about the Vril Society, wishing Walt were there to fully explain about them properly.

"We managed to get back to Brinnon and then came here. We were told that the kidnapping wasn't going to take place until tomorrow afternoon. It seems they have stepped up their plans." He turned to the director standing behind him and asked, "What happened?"

He stepped forward closer to the microphone on the table. "For those who came in late, I'll cover the incident today. The president and Senator Gregg decided to tour the city. They were just coming out of the downtown area and stopped at a Starbucks. While they were still outside the building this very large black airship flew up and stopped above the men. Numerous canisters of flash grenades suddenly fell from the ship and blinded everyone. A few men who hadn't seen the flash or felt the stun explosions saw two men lowered on cables from the ship who grabbed the president. Before the secret service realized what was happening, the men were pulled back up. They didn't shoot for fear of hitting the president."

He turned back to Warren. "You have nothing else on the airship?"

"Not any more than what I told you. We couldn't find the thing while it was on the ground. Even the Air Force and their spy planes couldn't find it," Warren replied. "After we knew there would be an attempt to grab the president we came right back."

The director spoke to the people in the room again. "Okay, we need to gather as much intel as we can on this

Fatal Abductions

Vril Society and get our lab guys scanning the ship above us. We need to know what they are up to. Now go. We don't know how much time the thing will be up there."

The room cleared in seconds as everyone went to do their jobs. The director turned to Warren. "What do you need to find out anything on that base back in Brinnon? They may head back there."

"Another helicopter to get us back there quickly would help," Warren said, hoping the director wouldn't blow up because they had lost two choppers already.

"I'll ignore the other two choppers. Just find out what you can. Do you think they could have another base out there?"

"They spent most of their time out there. And the base had to be used for something to carry out their plan."

As they stood talking an agent came running in and said loudly, "The airship is moving out of the city. It's heading west."

Dave and Warren looked at each other. Dave spoke first. "Heading in the direction of Brinnon."

The director said, "Okay, you have a chopper. But it's the last we have so don't screw it up. I'll have someone go with you with the necessary parts to fix the other choppers. Get these bastards."

"I'm sure the full force of the Army and Air Force will be tripping over themselves to follow it along with the

Secret Service. I hope they don't get in the way," Warren said.

Another agent came into the room and said that they had communications again. The phones and radios were working.

"I would have thought they would wait longer on that," Warren said.

"It's good. Now I can talk to the vice-president and explain that you have a jump on this. Maybe he'll have the military reel back on attacking. We need to get the president back in one piece. Now get out of here."

Warren led Dave out of the room and to the area where they kept the choppers. Warren pulled his cell phone and called Walt. It rang but there was no answer. "I hope Walt is alright."

"Let me try Sarah," Dave said and made a call to her. He got no answer. "Maybe the phones are still out over in Brinnon."

"Or that ship is what's causing the disturbance. When it moved away, we got our communications back. It could be blocking calls between us and Brinnon," Warren said.

"Whatever. By air we'll be back in Brinnon in about twenty minutes."

"If the ship doesn't shoot us down," Dave said with a smile.

"Shut up. Let's get out of here."

Fatal Abductions

Warren had explained to the chopper pilot about what wiring was removed from the other chopper. The pilot grabbed a few parts and got into the chopper. They flew up and were on the way.

"Keep low so we don't run into the ship," Warren warned.

"I've got it on my radar. I'll keep my distance," the pilot said.

"You can see it on your radar?" Warren asked.

"Yep, big and right ahead of us."

"Think you can follow it without being seen?" Warren asked.

"I'll try. If I can't get a visual on it, we'll have to follow it by radar," the pilot said.

"I would think with everything it can do, it could see us following them," Dave said from the back of the chopper.

"Well, maybe they don't care. But until they try and shoot us down, we'll follow," Warren said with a smile.

They were about five minutes from the shore of the canal by Brinnon when the pilot said, "That's strange. It vanished from the radar."

"Are you sure?" Warren asked.

"No, I'm kidding. Of course it's gone. They just dropped down and vanished."

"Dropped down? Where?" Warren asked.

"Well, since we are still over the canal, I'd say into the water," the pilot offered.

"Hot crap. The thing is submersible?" Warren asked.

"Seems that way. Unless the waters opened and took it in," the pilot said.

"Fly around a bit more and see if you can pick up anything."

The pilot flew the chopper in circles over the area and couldn't get a fix on the ship. "Nope, it's gone," he said.

"Okay, head to Dave's house where the first chopper is. Then we'll go to the ghost town," Warren said.

His cell phone rang, surprising him. He looked at the caller ID and saw it was Walt. "Hey, Walt, you got through. How is everyone holding up?" He put the speaker on so Dave could hear.

"We're holding up. I thought I'd try my phone and it works. Where are you?" Walt asked.

"We're just outside of Brinnon and heading to Dave's house. Did the equipment in your van come up with anything interesting?"

Fatal Abductions

"There are more tunnels here. We managed to break through one cave wall with the bazooka and found more labs. No people, but lots of equipment. They have been busy here for a long time, judging by the logs I found dating back to 1976."

"Okay, are you being fed?"

"The kitchen here is stocked and one of our agents used to be a cook in a restaurant. So he's fed us," Walt replied.

"Good. We should be out there shortly as soon as we solve a mystery here. We lost the airship and it seems to have dropped into the water of the canal."

"Submersible? It makes sense, I guess. We couldn't find it on land. But that doesn't make sense either. The thing is a blimp and couldn't go underwater with all that helium inside. It would float. Are you sure it went underwater?" Walt asked.

"At this point I think it could have entered another dimension. Oh, and it has the president aboard. They got him, Walt."

*

Chapter 24

They were just outside of Brinnon when two jets flew by them overhead. "Damn, they're still following. I'm sure they didn't get a fix on the airship like we did," Warren said.

"I hope they aren't going to get itchy fingers and start firing on us," Dave said.

"Larry, give them a call and warn them," Warren said to the pilot. He got on the radio and called. The jet pilots agreed not to fire indiscriminately and Warren said to tell them that the ship had vanished. They said they lost contact with the ship before they came into Brinnon airspace. The jet pilots radioed back that they got word to return to base and the men in the chopper could see them heading back.

"Okay, we have a chance to find the president without starting a war. Now we just need to find the damn ship," Warren said and frowned.

The chopper landed at Dave's home and the pilot went to the disabled chopper to see if he could fix it. Sarah and Alex came out of the house to Dave and Warren.

"Have you saved the world yet?" Sarah asked.

"Nope, and it got worse. The president of the U.S. was kidnapped by the alien ship," Dave said and kissed Sarah.

Fatal Abductions

"Are they going to probe him?" she said, trying not to laugh.

"This is serious. There never has been a president kidnapped in history other than in the movies," Dave said.

"Well, do what they did in the movies and get him back," she said.

Dave looked at Warren. "Do you remember how they saved the president?"

"I remember 'Air Force One' when they saved Harrison Ford. That's the only one I remember. But he did most of the saving," Warren replied. "Now we have to get on the airship and cause a diversion. Hopefully the president will attack his attackers."

"I'm not counting on that. We still need to find the ship," Dave said.

"If this new pilot can get the choppers going, we'll have three in the air looking."

The pilot came up to them and said, "This bird is going to need some major replacement to the control rods. You said the other just had its wiring ripped out?"

"Yep, other than that it should be good to fly," Warren said.

"Okay, as soon as we can get there, I'll fix it." He turned and went back to the chopper.

"We've wasted enough time, so let's get moving," Warren said. They went to the chopper after Dave gave Sarah a kiss and smiled at Alex. "Hopefully we'll get your brother back soon."

They were in the air and heading to the ghost town. About ten minutes later they landed. Walt was standing by with Harris and Sam.

"Got some parts to fix your chopper, Sam," Warren told the pilot. Sam and Harris went to the other pilot to work on the chopper.

"So you found more tunnels?" Warren asked Walt.

"Yes, they look like machine and wood shops. Probably where they worked on parts for the ship. Oh, and our phones are dead again," Walt said.

Warren looked surprised. "Now why would they suddenly work and not now?"

"When we lost track of the ship, the phones worked. Now they're out again. Maybe the ship is back. If it's the cause of the disturbances," Dave said.

"That's as good an explanation as any. As soon as the choppers are ready we'll head out. It's late and dark out but maybe we'll find the damn thing floating around."

They went to the pilots who were still hooking up the wiring harness. Sam looked back at the two men and said, "Luckily whoever did this just reached in and pulled out wires. The harness detached and didn't break anything. We'll have this harness in shortly."

181

Fatal Abductions

"What's your plan, chief?" Dave asked Warren.

"Plan? I was hoping you'd come up with something," he said with a smile.

"Does Walt have anything in his van that could detect large objects?" Dave asked.

"I'm sure he does. I'll ask." Warren went to where Walt was standing by his van and said, "Walt, you got any magic in the van that can find the ship?"

"I was thinking that if the ship is putting out some kind of jamming beam, I may be able to track it." He climbed into the van and brought out a box with dials and switches. He turned on a switch and the box lit up and made noises. "Well, since the ship got back from Seattle, this thing is working now. I have a reading on some powerful frequency being beamed all around. It has to be our blockage."

"Can you find out where it's coming from?" Warren asked.

Walt moved away from the van holding the box in front of him and moved it around him, circling the area. "It seems to be coming from the direction of the other side of the town."

"But there's a sheer wall there. It's a dead end," Dave said.

"It has to be on the other side of the rock wall," Walt said.

"It's all mountain top from what we saw when we flew over it yesterday. Maybe there's some opening where the ship went in." Warren turned to the pilots and asked, "How long before the thing is operational?"

Sam said, "It'll be about a half hour to make sure we got everything hooked up right. Then to test it. I wouldn't want to be up in the air and have a wire come loose."

"Okay, Harris, you come with us while they work. We'll need to fly up over this mountain to check something."

Harris went to the new chopper and started it up as Warren, Dave and Walt got in. They flew up and over to the mountain wall looming high behind the town. Harris crested the top and hovered over the surface.

Walt adjusted his box, said to move forward and pointed the direction. They went slowly as Walt was directing their movement across the fairly flat mountain top. "The signal seems to be strongest here. It has to be below us inside the mountain," Walt said.

Suddenly they saw a crack of light coming out from an opening on the side of the flat part of the mountain. In the pale moonlight they could see the ground was moving.

"What the hell?" Warren yelled. "The top of the mountain is opening. Harris, move us away before they see us."

The pilot veered off to the left over by a small peak in the mountain. They could see where the ground was moving towards them and Harris found a safe spot to land.

Fatal Abductions

"Shut her down so they don't hear the chopper," Warren told Harris.

He killed the engines and they sat watching the fake ground move over more.

"It's a covering made of some material like canvas. See where it's rolling up over there," Dave said, pointing.

They could see down into the hole revealed by the roof almost all the way open. There was the large black ship resting on the ground. The area around the ship was lit by work lights.

"Give Sarah a big kiss. She was right," Warren said with a grin. "It was in the mountain."

Walt spoke up, "No, it's in another valley and they have the canvas running across and over the valley. That way they didn't have to dig out a hole. From the sky the covering looked like the top of the mountain. I'm sure the covering is made of some kind of metal weave to block any attempts to probe the ground by our planes."

They got out of the chopper and went to the edge of the opening. Looking down they could see people moving about the outside of the ship. There were men detaching hoses from the ship. "Probably pumping in helium," Walt said. They watched as a troop of soldiers marched by the airship with six people between them. One was a small boy.

"Damn, it's Jeffery!" Dave said. "He's still alive and so is George."

"There's our agent Michaels and probably all the other kidnap victims from the Seattle area. Where are they taking them?" Warren asked.

"Probably from one area in the base to another in the mountain. But where's the president?" Walt asked.

They waited as there was a flurry of people running around. The ship suddenly started to shift and lift.

"They're taking it up again. The president must still be aboard. I didn't see them take him out," Warren said.

The ship slowly rose up and was very close to the edge where the men were hiding. There was a huge gondola attached to the bottom of the balloon that made up the biggest portion of the airship. On the outside of the gondola there was a walkway all around the outside. There were rails and beams attaching to ribs in the balloon.

Warren looked at Dave and said, "Are you thinking what I'm thinking?"

"I hope not. It could be dangerous if you're thinking what I think you're thinking," Dave replied.

"We better move fast or it will be out of range." They stood as Warren told Walt to fly back to the town and get the other agents to see if they could rescue the kidnapped people.

Warren and Dave went out to a jagged rock jutting out towards the ship as it slowly rose.

"I'll jump first then grab you," Warren said. He looked down and saw that it was a very long drop. He had to jump far to get to the walkway. He estimated farther than he had ever jumped. "Say a prayer," he said then leapt out, grabbing one of the lower rails of the walkway. He hung on for dear life then swung his leg up and over. Pulling himself up, he stood and ran down the walkway to where Dave was ready to jump as the blimp moved forward.

Dave took a big breath and jumped. He nearly missed the rail but Warren had hold of his arm and pulled with all his strength. Dave kicked as he tried to get his leg up and over the rail. Warren gave another pull and got Dave up and over.

*

Chapter 25

The two men stood looking down at the great distance to the ground that was now getting further away.

"I hope I never, ever have to do that again," Warren said breathlessly. "Let's see if we can get into this monstrosity."

They crept along the walkway until they came to windows in the front. Lowering down they peeked into the room and saw a number of men around a control panel looking out to the night sky. They had large radar screens and banks of computer monitors showing the details of the land below.

"They could run visually blind and still guide this thing around," Warren said. "I don't see the president. He must be in another part of the gondola."

They watched for a few minutes until a door at the back of the room opened and in walked a man in uniform. Warren made a small noise then said, "He's a Nazi. Walt mentioned that the Third Reich was interested in this Vril Society. Maybe they teamed back up after all these years."

"Nazis and aliens. Any more surprises?" Dave spoke softly. The men inside were talking but Warren couldn't hear. The wind around the blimp was loud and making it hard to hear. "Let's explore," he said and they turned towards the back of the ship. They came to a door and Warren slowly opened it. Peeking in, he saw no one nearby, just a hallway.

They entered the hallway as Dave said, "I hope they're busy in other parts of the ship. I don't want to walk into anyone, especially since we didn't bring any extra weapons."

"Well, I can't think of everything," Warren said with a smile. They heard voices from behind a door at the end of the hall. Warren signaled Dave to go into a door next to the end of the hall. Dave opened the door and found it was a closet containing cleaning supplies. They went in.

The door at the end of the hall opened and in came two soldiers in Nazi uniforms. Warren watched through a crack in the door as the soldiers stopped by the door, talking.

"We need disguises, and they look about our sizes." He smiled and opened the door. "Excuse me, but could we talk to you in here?" he said to the men. The soldiers gave a shocked look and ran to the door. There was a scuffle and both soldiers were knocked out. Dave used a wooden toilet scrubber to knock one of the men out.

"Nice weapon. I just used my superior strength and a lucky punch," Warren said. They stripped the men and changed into the uniforms.

"It feels so wrong wearing this uniform. My dad fought these people in the war," Dave said.

"It's just to be able to get around without causing suspicion. As soon as we find the president, we can get out of them." Warren picked up the rifles the soldiers had. "Now we have extra weapons. Are you happy now?"

"I'm overjoyed. Let's get out of here. This room stinks." They went out into the hall again and went back to the door where the soldiers came out from. Warren opened it and walked in like he knew where he was going. He didn't.

They were in a large room with about a dozen other soldiers standing around a table as an officer was giving them orders.

"We have a duty to guard this airship to our death. We will help our Vril friends to take over the world starting with the United States then moving out to the rest of the world. We will indoctrinate the masses to our way, even if it's one country at a time."

Warren and Dave were at the back of the room listening. "These people are nuts," Warren said to Dave quietly.

"Now I'm assigning four of you men to guard the president. Do not let anything happen to him. He's our safe card to get to Washington to blow up the government buildings with all the evil men that occupy the government." He pointed to four men and told them to go. They went through another door as the officer said, "The rest of you patrol the ship. Go!"

The men all went in different directions as Dave and Warren headed to the door where the president's guards went. No one gave them a second look. Warren checked back to see if anyone was watching them, but everyone was busy with their own jobs.

Warren went through the door and it was another small hallway. They went to each door, opening and checking the rooms. They came to the last door and found it to be a room that was made up like a lounge. Warren saw the four guards sitting around the president who was tied in a chair, his mouth covered by tape.

Warren walked in followed by Dave and said to the closest soldier, "The captain wants to see you and you." He pointed to two men. "We'll take over."

The men didn't even blink, just walked out. Dave whispered to Warren, "That was too easy."

Fatal Abductions

"I know, but we are in the room without getting shot," Warren whispered back.

One of the soldiers came up and looked Warren in the face. "I don't know you. Who are you?"

"I'm the man who's going to knock you out," Warren said, brought up the butt of his rifle and knocked the man down. Dave went to the other man and put his gun in the man's face. The soldier put his hands up.

"These neo-Nazis aren't very brave, are they?" Dave said.

Warren went up to the man and punched him out. The soldier went down. Warren and Dave went to the president who was looking worried.

"Mr. President, I'm Special Agent Warren Stevens, FBI. This man is Sheriff Dave Chandler from Brinnon, Washington. We're here to save you." Warren carefully pulled the tape from the president's mouth.

The man looked relieved and said, "You're all that's here? Don't you have an army behind you?"

"Mr. President, we were lucky to have found the ship. There was no time to bring in the marines. Besides, our phones aren't working. We can't call for help. We need to get out of here ASAP," Warren said quickly. The president stood and Warren said they had to make a plan.

The president said, "They brought me through that door from what looked like a hanger with a couple small planes. If we can get in there maybe we can fly out."

Warren looked at the president and said, "Do you fly? I can't and neither can the sheriff."

"Yes, Agent, I can fly, and damn well. Let's get the hell out of here."

Warren picked up the rifles from the soldiers on the floor. He handed one to the president and they went to the door. Warren held the president back and said, "I have to protect you, so you don't go playing cowboy. I'll do that."

The president smiled and waved Warren towards the door. "After you," he said.

Warren opened the door and carefully looked in. There were two small planes tethered to the floor as a couple men were working on a helicopter towards the other side of the room. Warren could see that the back of the room was actually a huge door that he presumed went to the outside of the gondola. He straightened and said to follow his lead. "Mr. President, put your hands behind your back and pretend you are our prisoner. Dave, take his weapon."

Warren opened the door and they went into the hanger. The workmen looked over and saw Warren in uniform so they ignored him and went back to work.

"So far so good," Warren said as they approached the first plane closest to the outer door. "There's not much of a runway here. As a matter of fact there is no runway at all."

The president spoke quietly, "If you can get the door open I'll do a dead drop take off."

Fatal Abductions

Warren stared at him and said, "I hope you know what you're talking about. I'll trust you."

"Find out how they open the door," Warren said to Dave. Dave went to the wall and found a control panel on the side. It said open and close. He figured it must be what they needed.

One of the mechanics came over and asked what they were doing.

Warren put his gun in the man's face and said, "Well, you tell us that. We need to fly this plane out the door so if you help, I won't kill you. Otherwise kiss your ass good-bye."

The man gave a panicked look and said not to kill him. "I'm just a worker, not a soldier. I don't care if you get out. Fine, I'll help."

"Good. Do we need a key?" he asked the president.

"No, this plane has push controls to start." He got in the pilot's seat and pushed a few buttons. The plane kicked in and started. The other workers came running over but Dave had his rifle aimed at them. They stopped.

"On the ground. All of you, now!" Dave yelled over the engine of the plane. Warren covered the men as Dave released the tethers holding the plane to the floor. Then he went to the control panel again to open the hanger door. He threw the switch but nothing happened. He ran back to the man still standing, pushed his gun in the man's face and yelled, "Open the damn thing now!"

Chapter 26

The man fumbled in his pocket and came out with a key. Dave pushed him to the control panel and told him to turn it on. The man put the key in and turned it. The panel lit up and then he pulled the switch to open the door.

There was a loud noise caused by air rushing in from the outside. Dave told the man to get down and he went to the plane. Warren was already inside.

The hangar door opened further as they suddenly heard gun fire. They looked back and saw soldiers flowing into the hangar with weapons firing. "Damn, we have to get out of here," Dave said.

The president said, "The door isn't open enough. Another minute."

Dave and Warren smashed out the plane's rear windows and started to fire. "Now, Mr. President. There's more soldiers coming in."

The door wasn't fully open but the president gunned the engine and let the plane move forward. There was just barely enough headroom for the plane going out the door, but it wasn't a time to wait. The plane shot out of the back of the gondola as soldiers came up, still firing.

The plane went into a dive straight down and the president was doing his best to bring the nose up. Dave was sitting in the second seat and the president yelled to pull on the steering column. Dave put all he could into pulling back on the controller. The plane was getting dangerously close to the ground.

Warren said to Dave, "Think of Sarah and pull on the son-of-a-bitch."

The plane arced and finally the nose came up. The president told Dave he could release the wheel. Dave had to pry his hand off the thing.

All was quiet in the cockpit as the plane sailed along just above the ground.

"Mr. President," Dave said, "I'd be careful. This area is all mountains. I'd hate to think we escaped to crash into the side of a hill."

The president laughed out loud. Warren and Dave joined him. They were all relieved that they escaped and the laughter helped to release the tension.

It was quiet again. The president said, "Thank you, men. I owe you my life. I'm sure my wife will be relieved that I'm alive. Where do we go now?"

Warren said, "I haven't the faintest idea how to tell you to get back to Brinnon. Maybe we can fly right into Seattle to save travel time."

The president checked the fuel gauge and said, "We have enough fuel to get there. Think it would be a good idea?"

"Well, all your men are there. I think it's a safe bet they might want to see you," Dave said.

"Mr. President, did you hear anything that they said as to what they were going to do?" Warren asked.

"Call me Steve. You deserve that," he said. "The leader of the group was very open and bragging about his desire to rule everything. He was a total fruitcake. He said they have a weapon that was created years ago by the Vril Society. It could knock out communications and the weapon was powerful enough to destroy buildings and cities. Once they had me aboard they planned on flying to Washington, D.C., and destroying the Capital building along with the Senate and the House. Total chaos. They figured no one would fire on them as long as I was aboard. Now if we could get word back and have them blown out of the sky."

Dave pulled his cell phone and it was still dead.

"They won't let us call for help. We'll just have to make it back to Seattle. I don't have a flight plan but I think I can get us there," the president said.

Dave was watching the ground. It was starting to get light out as the sun was coming up. Dave yelled that he knew where they were. "We're right by the ghost town. We can land on the road and change over to the chopper. It has GPS." Warren agreed. Dave guided the president to where the road that led to the town was and they landed safely. The president taxied the plane down the road and up to the town. They could see Walt and the new pilot by only one chopper.

They stopped the plane and got out. Walt was surprised to see the president.

Fatal Abductions

"Is the chopper ready to fly?" Warren asked the pilot. He said it was.

Dave asked, "Did you try to get the hostages out?"

"We went back up, but there were too many soldiers. Did you know there are Nazis up there? Sam took his chopper and flew back to Seattle to bring reinforcements."

"Are you talking about the men they kidnapped?" the president asked.

"Yes, they're still in the base over that hill," Dave said, pointing.

"The bastards had a child. We need to get them out," the president said.

"You need to get safely back to Seattle, sir."

"Bull hockey. We'll get those people out first. I got to meet them briefly. We need to save them and the child."

"What do you want to do, sir? You're now in charge," Warren said.

"How many men do you have?" he asked.

Warren turned to Walt. "How many are still here?"

Walt made a mental count and said six.

"Are all the weapons still in the chopper?" Warren asked, and Walt said they were.

"Sir, we have weapons enough to blast them out. Plus this chopper has rockets that can knock out any large target," Warren said.

"Good. I can't do anything back in Seattle. Let's get moving." He went to the chopper as the men followed. They all packed into the chopper. Walt loaded the bazooka on board.

Warren asked Walt, "Do you know how to operate this thing?"

"If he doesn't, I do," the president said. "I was in the infantry and used a number of those."

Walt nodded and climbed into the chopper. The pilot started it up and flew back up the way to the base.

It was getting light out and they hoped they wouldn't be spotted. The helicopter set down where it landed earlier, away from the canvas cover which was closed now. Walt led the men to where they could crawl under the canvas on the side.

There were numerous men running around down in the bottom of the valley. The men climbed carefully down a trail on the side and made it to the bottom of the hill.

Warren came to the president and said, "Sir, Steve, you really need to stay behind us, in case. The U.S. needs you more than these people."

Dave said, "Sir, these people are friends of ours. We'll get them out. It's a priority. But we can't replace you."

Fatal Abductions

The man stood watching the faces of the men before him. "Okay, but I want a shot at them too. So keep your heads down if I'm behind you."

They turned from behind the cover they had off the side and studied the area. There were about ten people milling about and none of them were armed. Unfortunately there were a few soldiers patrolling the area. They moved along one side behind a row of trucks and heavy equipment. They came to the doors in the side of the hill most likely leading to their quarters.

Warren and Dave told the agents to hold back since they were still wearing the Nazi uniforms. They moved out and tried to look like they fit in. They went to the first door and opened it. There was a room filled with many boxes that were labeled ammo. The room seemed to be a dead end so they went to the next door. It was a much bigger room and in the center there was a cage. It held the hostages.

Warren looked back and could see Walt peeking around the boxes on the side. He studied the landing area. Most of the men were busy doing their jobs and the few soldiers were milling around in a group having a smoke.

Warren signaled to his men and they came running to the door and in. There was no one else in the room except the hostages. They went to the cage and George looked stunned. "The president?" he said.

"Yes, George, it's him. Now get back while I blast the cage lock," Dave said. "Be ready everyone, this is going to bring trouble when I fire."

"Wait!" Agent Michaels yelled. "The key is hanging over there," he said, pointing to a post with the key on the side.

"Now that takes the fun out of it," Dave said to Warren and went to get the key. He opened the door and everyone came out. "George, take charge of the boy," he said. The cop said he'd help George.

They went back to the door just as three of the soldiers were approaching. "Crap, wait until they get in here. Then grab them," Warren said to his men. They stood along the wall by the door as the soldiers entered and were pounced on by the agents. A small fight ensued but ended quickly.

They tied up the three men with ropes they found nearby and then went to the door again. Warren looked out carefully. There were about a dozen soldiers gathered in the center of the yard. Warren couldn't see what they were doing but hoped they wouldn't see the men run to the side.

They made a break for cover but found soldiers hiding behind the boxes they were heading for. The others in the yard came running up with weapons out. The men were surrounded by soldiers.

"Crap, and we were so close," Warren said.

*

Chapter 27

The soldiers filed across the men with weapons aimed towards them. A man in an officer's uniform came up from behind the men and up to Warren and Dave.

"Did you think you would escape us? We have eyes everywhere watching every move on this base. We knew where you were and what you were up to."

"Still testing your security?" Michaels yelled.

"Of course, Agent Michaels. We caught you before and we caught you now. You're not very resourceful."

The officer walked down the row of agents and was surprised to see the president. "I don't believe it. How did you get back here?"

"Sloppy work by your men on the blimp," the president replied.

"Well, I'm going to have a long talk with them. We need to get you back on the ship. I'll send a message to them and they will unfortunately have to turn back."

Warren smiled. "I think they already know they lost the president."

"Well, I think we need to get rid of you pests." He took the president away from the others and told his men to execute the rest of the agents.

Bob Moats

The soldiers raised their weapons just as there was a huge explosion from above. The canvas covering above them had a large hole blown in it and the thing was starting to flame up. From the large hole, now getting bigger, the men on the ground could see the helicopter lowering into the valley. It turned and fired one of the rockets at the line of trucks causing huge explosions from their gas tanks.

Warren and the others ran to the side as the soldiers scattered to run for cover. The helicopter turned again and fired another rocket into a number of boxes along one wall away from the agents' escape. Then the chopper went back up out of the hole which was growing larger, flaming bits of canvas and metal coming down on the ground.

Warren and his people ran back up the trail to the top of the mountain. At the top they found the chopper resting, waiting for them. They piled on and the pilot took off.

Warren sat in the seat next to the pilot and said, "One more thing. Turn back into the valley and see if you can spot a door on the right side of the hill. Fire a rocket at that door."

The pilot turned in and aimed at the door that Warren was pointing out. He fired another rocket and it flew towards the door. Warren yelled to move away quickly. The pilot veered away as the rocket made contact with the room that Warren saw earlier containing ammo. The side of the wall exploded in a huge ball of flame taking out most of the rock wall, collapsing the entire side of the mountain wall.

Fatal Abductions

"Let's get out of here and call in the marines to clean up," Warren said with a big smile of satisfaction.

They arrived back at the ghost town just as a fleet of choppers were streaming across the sky led by Sam in his chopper. They all landed on the road by the plane, and the ten transport choppers parked. A couple hundred military men along with agents of the FBI and secret service were streaming out.

The secret service came up to the president and stood by guarding him. An army colonel came marching up to the president and saluted. The president returned salute and explained to the colonel where to go to find the base. The officer gathered his men, got back into the choppers and flew over the hill to the base.

"It's their show now," Warren said to Dave. They stood in the road, happy to be alive. Dave went to Jeffery, looking excited by all the activity going on around him. Dave leaned down and said, "Jeff, your brother is at my house waiting for you. We'll take you there as soon as we finish here."

"No rush, sheriff, I'm enjoying this," the boy said with a big smile.

Dave ruffled his hair and told George to keep an eye on him. Dave went to Warren standing by the president. "We still don't have communications but as soon as we can knock the monster out of the sky, we'll be all right," the president said.

They could hear gun fire from over the hill and Dave said, "That should finish the base."

They stood congratulating everyone on a job well done. Warren went to the pilot of the chopper that saved them and said, "I don't even know your name."

"It's Special Agent Ted West."

"Well, Ted, you saved our butts back there. They were going to execute us just as you blew the place to hell," Warren said.

"I was watching from above. When I saw what they were going to do I just couldn't let that happen. I had weapons and used them."

"You did good. I'll see you get a citation for this." He turned and called Michaels over. "I'll need your report as to what happened after they took you, but I'll see you get a commendation for your part."

Dave went and sat on a chair in the middle of the road that was used by Warren to scare the prisoners. He sighed and said to himself, "Sarah's never going to believe me on this."

About an hour later the military was examining the base and cleaning up. Prisoners were taken and held until they could be transported out of the valley. Without communications the going was slow.

The president was taken back to Seattle after he thanked everyone for his rescue. He told Warren and Dave that they would be brought out to Washington to the White House for a ceremony and dinner. Dave thought that Sarah would like that.

Fatal Abductions

All that was left was to find the blimp that had disappeared again. Since the president wasn't aboard, the blimp was fair game to be shot down.

Warren and Dave didn't care. It was the military's problem now. Warren gathered all his men by one of the choppers that Sam was in charge of and had them fly back to Seattle. Harris and Ted West were waiting to transport the rest of the men back to Brinnon. Walt had already left with the van to get a jump on the time it would take to get to Brinnon. He took Virgil with him for company. The prisoners in the town were all taken away by the military, and the extra FBI agents who showed up left with the transport choppers.

The town was a ghost town once more. Warren and Dave stood on the road looking at the mess.

"The military is going to permanently seal the tunnel once they examine everything inside. I hope they find Hitler's brain in there. He sure didn't use it," Warren said with a laugh. "Okay, you've had serial killers, terrorists, zombies, drug dealers and now aliens. Think it's time to move?"

"I think Sarah would like to move to Las Vegas. But I'm just an old country sheriff and happy with my life. Well, other than all those people you mentioned. I don't know how many times we can be invaded by bad guys. It has to hit a saturation point and stop. I'll take speeders through Brinnon any day," Dave said and went to the chopper followed by Warren.

They loaded George and Jeffery on the chopper. The other hostages went back with the transports to Seattle.

Harris and Ted were in the front seats and ready to leave the ghost town for good. The chopper flew up and headed to Brinnon.

As the chopper was touching down in Dave's front yard, Sarah and Alex were waiting. As soon as the chopper settled, the door opened and Jeffrey jumped out and ran straight to Alex. The boys hugged and Alex lifted his brother and swung him around.

"Shall I swing you around too?" Dave asked Sarah as he hugged her.

"Gee, I don't get to hug anyone," Warren said, looking sad. Sarah came over and gave him a hug.

Walt and Virgil were coming up the road and pulled into the yard. "That was timed well," Warren said and went to his partner. He gave the surprised young man a hug also.

Walt asked, "What was that for?"

"Everyone else was doing it. You needed a hug too." Warren laughed and went to the pilots.

"You hug me and I'll hit you," Harris said. "I don't care if you are the senior agent out here, you don't hug me."

Warren laughed, stood back and watched the pilots working on the first chopper. Sam had brought back a new rod to fix the thing when he came back with the troops. Harris and Ted were busy working to fix it.

Dave and Sarah went to the boys and Dave said, "We need to get you back to your mother. I can't call her since the phones still aren't working so we'll drive you there." Then he realized his Bronco was still in Seattle. "We'll have to take a trip out to get my car," he said to Sarah.

"Do you have to take us to our mother? I'd like to stay here," Alex said.

"Well, we have to take you back, but I'll see some people who may help you with your problem. Hang in there until you hear from me," Dave said to the boy.

"I'm hungry. Is anyone else hungry?" Warren said, coming up with Walt.

"You're always hungry. I'll put some burgers on the grill," Dave said.

*

Chapter 28

Everyone sat enjoying the burgers from the grill and Sarah even whipped up a salad. Not having a phone was pleasant. It cut off people from bothering you.

Mike pulled into the drive and got out of the patrol car. "Nice of you to invite me," he said when he saw the food.

Dave told him to come get a burger. "How's everyone in town surviving without phone service?"

"It's a mess. People are pouring into the station with complaints that they would normally call in. I finally had to get away and came here to see if anything has changed. When did you get back?" Mike asked.

"About an hour and a half ago. We needed food, so I threw together a BBQ. I would have invited you, but the phones aren't working," Dave said.

"Neither is my radio. It's been deathly quiet today."

"It's starting to get dark, so you and Virgil decide who is going to man the station for the night. I'm flying back with the choppers to get my car in Seattle in a while."

Mike looked over to Jeffrey. "You found the boy I see. And George, too."

"Yep, could you drive George back to his wife? I think he's had enough to eat."

"Sure, after I get my food eaten," Mike said with a grin.

Everyone was cleaning up from the makeshift picnic. Mike and Virgil drove George back home and said they'd be back. Dave went to the boys who were playing with Van Gogh and asked the boys if they'd like to spend one more night at his house.

"I'll take you back in the morning. You two can get some good rest tonight," he said.

"Yeah, that would be nice," Alex said. They ran off with the dog following.

Fatal Abductions

Warren came up and said, "Walt is going to take the van back and I'm flying with you to Seattle to get your car. Are you ready?"

"In a minute," he said and went to Sarah. He gave her a good lip lock and said in her ear, "I love you." She returned the sentiment and Dave said he was going.

They went to the chopper as Harris was getting it ready. Ted fired up the repaired chopper and flew off. Warren was aboard and helped Dave up. Dave gave Sarah one last look and a wave then closed the door. Sarah moved back as the chopper revved up and then ascended.

She watched the chopper move away as she saw a strange black object in the now darken sky coming up behind the chopper. She knew what it was and ran to the boys, telling them to get in the house. She cursed the fact that she had no way to call Dave and warn him.

The men were relaxing in the chopper as it flew back to Seattle.

"Well, we have something to tell our grandchildren now," Warren said with a laugh.

"You have to have children first before you can have grandchildren," Dave said.

"Damn!" Harris yelled. "We're being followed."

"What!" Warren exclaimed and looked back out the window. He could barely see it, but it was the airship. "How the hell did it find us?" he said.

Dave could just make it out also and said, "Maybe they didn't find us. Maybe they're heading to Seattle, too, and we're in their way."

"Harris, get out of the way. They're too close," Warren told the man.

Harris banked away from the path of the ship and came back around behind it.

"For being such a fantastic machine, they sure don't know what's going on around them," Harris said. "They haven't even tried to fire on us."

"I don't remember any outside weapons, do you?" Warren asked Dave.

"Just the walkway around the gondola. Maybe they fire from there with hand weapons," Dave said.

As they were watching they could barely see light from a door opening and men came out on the walkway. Suddenly there was a flash and a rocket was streaming towards them. "Bazooka!" Warren yelled as Harris was banking away from the rocket. "Those things don't have any guidance," Warren said.

"Screw this," Harris said. "My rockets have guidance." He flipped a switch. One of the missiles shot out from the pod below the chopper and flew directly toward the ship's gondola. They could see the men scatter as the rocket hit its target. The back side of the gondola where the hangar was exploded in a bright flash.

Fatal Abductions

"Hit the balloon next! That should take them down!" Warren yelled.

Harris fired another missile and it penetrated the balloon, exploding inside. The helium inside wasn't explosive but was leaking out through the hole caused by the explosion of the missile.

"David and Goliath!" Warren yelled. "They're going down!" Harris flew out around the side and they could see explosions inside the gondola. "The whole thing is blowing up!"

Dave pulled his cell phone and dialed Warren. Warren got a strange look when his phone buzzed. "Are you calling me?" he asked Dave.

"Just testing. We knocked out the jammer. You can call the military now and tell them where to find the ship," Dave said.

"Yeah, in the Hood Canal. We're over water now," Harris said.

"Okay, so call the Navy to come and fish it out," Dave said with a smile.

They watched it hit the water, barely able to see it other than the explosions.

Warren called the bureau and told them to call the appropriate people in charge to come get the thing. He hung up and said, "They can handle it now. We did our part."

Harris recorded the coordinates and Warren called again to give them to the person in charge. He hung up and said, "Maybe we can enjoy the rest of our ride now."

The chopper approached the landing field next to Ted and his chopper. They landed and the field crew came out to take care of getting the thing settled. Warren and Dave exited the craft and thanked Harris for all he did.

A car came driving up and out stepped another agent Warren knew. "Kent, are you our greeting party?" he asked.

"The director sent me to bring you in. You have a ton of reports to make," Kent said.

Warren looked at Dave and said, "I think it's that time I retire."

"The director got a call from the White House. Seems you made a very big friend," Kent added.

Warren smiled and said, "We go way back together. We fought in battle."

Dave stared at Warren and said, "You're an idiot." He was laughing as he went to the car.

An hour later Dave was on his way back to Brinnon. Warren had told stories of their bravery in the face of danger. Dave had to get away before the bullshit got too deep.

Fatal Abductions

He called Sarah who was happy to hear he was safe. "I saw that thing following behind you and I felt helpless to call. I'm glad you're alright and the thing is destroyed."

"I'll be home in another hour and we can celebrate. Do we have enough beer?"

"I'll make sure you have enough. My hero."

Dave pulled into the drive and parked. His phone buzzed and he saw by the caller ID it was Warren. "What now, another threat to my quiet existence?"

"Nope, just wanted to tell you we are invited to go to the White House for a special night. We are getting the Medal of Honor or some big deal award. I may make director one day soon."

"It might help your image. I'm home now. I'm going in to open about ten beers and collapse into my bed. I'm tired and I want to get away from you." He hung up on his friend and laughed.

Dave woke early and stretched. Sarah was already out of bed and he could hear noise from the kitchen. He went out and found her and the boys having breakfast.

"I didn't want to wake you. I let you sleep," she said

"Thank you," he said and kissed her. "We have to take the boys back to their mother. So when you're ready we'll go. I have to get back to work and soothe the nerves of my deputies."

Bob Moats

They ate their food and went out to the Bronco. Dave drove to Agnes' house and she came out to greet them. She latched onto Jeffrey then pulled Alex closer, hugging them both. "Thank you, sheriff, for bringing them back."

"Agnes, can I talk to you?" Dave asked and took the woman aside, out of earshot of the boys. "I'm only going to say this once. You start taking better care of your boys. Don't leave them alone at night and if I were you, I'd drop Dan quickly." She started to say something, but Dave stopped her. "I'm going to be checking regularly. If I see any problems, I'm taking the boys to child services to get them into a foster home. Do you understand?"

"I already got rid of Dan. He didn't care that the boys were gone. So I told him to hit the road."

"Good. Now Alex is a kid and he's without a good father. Give him the chance to prove that he's a good young man. Give him your time and he'll be alright."

"I will, sheriff, thank you," the woman said and turned back to her boys.

Dave and Sarah left and Dave drove to the station. They went in and found Virgil sitting at his desk.

"Did Mike go home?" Dave asked.

Mike came out of the conference room with powdered sugar on his chin, smiling.

Fatal Abductions

THE END

*

Thank you for purchasing this book. Your support keeps me writing. For more on my other books go to http://murdernovels.com Thanks, Bob Moats.

The Jim Richards series books by Bob Moats

(In series order)

"Classmate Murders"
"Vegas Showgirl Murders"
"Dominatrix Murders"
"Mistress Murders"
"Bridezilla Murders"
"Magic Murders"
"Strip Club Murders"
"Made-for-TV Murders"
"Mystery Cruise Murders"
"Talk Show Murders"
"Sin City Murders"
"Black Widow Murders"
"Vegas Vigilante Murders"
"Area 51 Murders"

Bob Moats

"Mortuary Murders"
"Hypnotic Murders"
"Sunshine State Murders"
"Blue Suede Murders"
"Honky Tonk Murders"
"Dark Carnival Murders"
"Lipstick Murders"
"Pasta Murders"
"Talent Show Murders"
"Shyster Murders"
"Campground Murders"
"Network Murders"
"Reunion Murders"
"Big Apple Murders"
"Kennel Murders"
"Trick or Treat Murders"
"Santa Murders"
"Wiseguy Murders"
"Toxic Murders"

The Fatal Series Books:
"Fatal Rejection"
"Fatal Departure"
"Fatal Romance"
"Fatal Outbreak"
"Fatal Abduction"

For more about Bob Moats books
go to http://murdernovels.com

What a few people are saying about the Murder Novels by Bob Moats

Mr. Moats, I just got your novel "Classmate Murders" and have to let you know, I read it in one evening. That is the first book I have ever done that with. That was the most enjoyable book I have ever read. I just started reading e-books, and reading again, after getting my wife a Kindle. This book was my 12th, and the best. I just got Las Vegas Showgirls to (read) tomorrow evening. ☺. I look forward to reading many of your books in this series. I have been searching for an author and books that were fun, entertaining reads. Your books are just the ticket.

Regards, A new fan, Bill from South Carolina

****

Hi Bob, I just had to write you... Last week I purchased a Nook Soft Touch e-reader. I was downloading free e-books and downloaded "Classmate Murders" from Barnes & Noble. I read it that night and enjoyed it so much that I went to search for the next one (as listed at end of the book). Read it and searched again. After reading the second one, I did a search from my e-reader for you and bought ALL of the books. So in the last week I have read all of the Jim Richards books. Finished the last one early this morning. I only read at night 10-6 when my neighbor is asleep. As I read the books I sometimes laughed and sometimes cried. I could relate to Jim as we are both in the 60s. I liked how "Jim" refers to previous murders in each book. That is great for anyone who has not read the books in order and also as fast as I did. Anyway, I just had to write and tell you how much I enjoyed the books.

Nancie S.

****

Another very nice comment submitted through my website from a person named Micki P.:

"I recently was given a kindle for my 60th birthday. The first book I downloaded was the Classmate Murders and have now read every one of the them. Today I started on the Fatal Rejection series. Thank you for the wonderful ride with Jim and Penny and all the rest of the troop. I have laughed and giggled thru the stories, my poor family gave me the strangest looks! Now I really want a little Yorkie!! Fatal Rejection so far is another great read! I will be looking out for more of Jim Richards and since you are my #1 Author, anything of yours I can find."

****

Received another comment on my books from Chanel:

Fatal Abductions

"On December 26th while playing around with my Kindle and looking for new and interesting books to read I happened upon Classmate Murders and decided to give it a whirl. Well, today is January 3, 2012, and I have since finished Classmate Murders and all that followed and am today starting Bridezilla Murders. I absolutely LOVE the characters and the way they all mesh. Jim and Penny are my heroes. I want to be in love like that when I am in my 60s. God bless and continued success. Thank you for providing such a roller-coaster of love, intrigue and mystery and showing that no matter how old you get you are not out of the game until you are "out" of it!"

****

Received a feedback form reply on my website from a Cassy B. Here's what she said:

"Well, I just finished all 22 of your novels. I certainly hope you are hard at work at your laptop. I haven't run straight through a series since John D. MacDonald's Travis McGee series. I thoroughly enjoy your characters, the plot twists and the humor in all your stories. Keep them coming!"

Jim Richards Family of Readers

Thanks to the following people who are now part of the Jim Richards Family of Readers. They have read a book or more and enjoyed them. They all volunteered to be included in the list. If you are a fan of the books, send me your name and you will be included in future books. Send your name to murdernovels@bobmoats.com to be added here and on the website.

* Achim Feifel * Al Norris * Alex Wheatley * Alexandra Delporte-Wilkinson * Amy Tapia * Andrea Bryan * Anne Shepherd * Arianda Sugar * Arlene Markowski * Ashley Augustus * Audra Hall * Barbara Hughes * Barbara Sammons * Barbara Schuler * Barbara Zirger * Beth Donohue Plenskofski * Beth Rosin * Betsy Childress * Beth Gibson * Bill Sandy * Bill Tornquist * Billie-jo Collie * Boni J Rychener * Candace Larson * Carl Bishopric * Carla Lewis * Carole Henderson * Carolyn Conroy * Carolyn Riddle-Linington * Cassy Bailey * Cathie Turner * Chad Hudson * Charlie Meier * Charlotte L Duran * Cheryl L. Everett * Cindy Ackley Nunn * Cindy Valstad * Connie Bancroft * Corinne Kay O'Daniel * Dana Robbins Chuchran * Dana Wichita * Daniel Kalus * Danielle Monique * Darren Heald * Dave Travers * David Wilkinson * DeAnn Jannereth * Deanna Miller * Deb Breuker Balbo * Debbie Carter * Debbie White * Deborah Fartuch * Deborah Gauze * Deborah Sullivan * Dee King * Denise Freeman * Diana Carver * Dixie Beck * Donna Gould * Donna Thompson * Donny Minter * Doris Kight * Eddie Moore * Eric Walters * Felicia Annette Bradfield * Francine Menor * Gail Chesney * Georgiann Minster * George Conner * Greg

Fatal Abductions

Colucci * Hayley Rankin * Harold Garcia * Heidi Arnold * Irma Ranee Coy * Jack Plunkitt * Jacqueline Moss * Jan Kimball * Jane Lawson * Janice Schneider * Janice Spoor * Jennifer Besner * Jennifer Redmond * Jerry Dornak * Jessica Keown-Belous * Jim Beck * Jo Boguslaw * Jo Turner * Joan Kimball * Joanne Marie Turner * John Peiffer * John Wisbiski * Joseph Wauro * Joyce Stacy * Joyce Trifiletti * Judy Franklin * Judy Travers * Judy Padgett * Julie Heath * Junnahvee Benson * Karen Dahl * Karen Grams * Karen Higham * Karen Kaiser * Karen Meinburg Richwine * Karen Kirkman Parker * Karin Hawkins * Karin Vasvari * Kathleen Donohue Roesing * Kathleen Riddle-Wolfe * Kathy Hinds Moore * Kathy Jones * Kathy Mitchell * Katie Benzler * Kay Burns * Kelly Garcia * Ken Boggs * Keota Rodriguez * Kiera Mccarthy * Kim Estes * Kimberley May * Kitty Stolle * Kristie Sciler * Kirsty Stanton * LaLonnie Scallen * Larry Morris * Leann Parr * Lenora Scales * Leslie Marie Jackson * Linda Forester * Linda Ingle Cox * Linda Kennerö * Linda Magill * Lisa Bower * Lisa Keller * Liz Gibson * Lorraine Wiman * Loretta Alexander * Lynda Bowles * Lynette Lawrance * LuAnn Louttit * Manny Rothman * Marcia Gibson DeWitt * Marie Calder * Marlene Bryan * MaryLouise Kramp * Mary Lynn Gross * Megan Atkins * Meghan Hyden * Melody Cannavan * Michael Carruthers * Michael Dinkens * Michael Vannoy * Michelle Burns-Mitchell * Michelle Pilcher * Micki Potter * Mike Moats * Mimi Baur * Myrna Hecht * Nadine Sutton * Nancy Ellen Sayre * Natalie Quine * Neena Martin * O'Della Wilson * Pat Pollington * Pat Rohn * Patricia Jarmon * Patricia C Trezza * Patrick Barry * Paul Lawrance * Peggy Davis * Phyllis Bassett * Raylene Matheny * Rebecca Collins Besner * Renee Brumley * Reta Hanna * Reta Moats * Robert Lenski * Roberta Navarro-Harder * Sally Berneathy * Sally Hubler

Bob Moats

* Sarah Santos * Satka Nikc * Sharon E. Edwards *
Sharon Mangini * Sharon McMillon * Sheena Rawl *
Sherry Amstutz * Shirley Alvarez * Shirley Davies *
Shirley Williams * Stacie Rowe * Stephanie Conner *
Steve Cullen * Susan Haughton * Susan Hesse Adams *
Susan Salomon * Suzan K Chase * Suzanne B. Bryere *
Taisha Cullum * Tamara Moore * Tammy Castleberry *
Tammy Lynn Wood * Ted Murphy * Terri Atkins * Terri
Creech * Terry Raab * Tonia Rachael Riggs-Williams *
Tonya Mann * Travis Fleury-Lopez * Twyla Gawlas *
Val Brooks * Walt Munsel * Yvonne Isakson *

Thank you for purchasing this book. I hope
you enjoy it as much as I enjoyed writing it
for my faithful readers. Please feel free to
email me to tell me what you thought about
my stories. I love hearing from the readers. I
can be reached at murdernovels@bobmoats.com
thanks again!